Sarah's Lot

SHIRLEY ANNE LYTTLE

For my loving father, Robert, who died August 2016. He is sorely missed.

ACKNOWLEDGEMENTS

Thanks to my Daughter-in-Law, Pippa, for her help in designing the cover of this book, my son, David, for all his publishing technical support, and last but not least, the characteristics contributed by my family and friends who brought the figures in Sarah's Lot to life.

CHAPTER ONE

Amelia Sharpe has many years of counselling experience in marriage guidance, eating disorders and depression. Here she recalls one of her more intriguing cases of a woman named Sarah, who, in November 2015, was, referred by her GP, for counselling.

Sarah was sixty-five years old, and seemed a very unhappy woman at that time. She looked forlorn, apathetic, and her hair was lifeless with no style. This surrounded a haggard-looking face, showing eyes which seemed devoid of life. She had retreated into her shell, and nothing held meaning for her. From the first moment Amelia met her she knew this woman desperately needed her help.

Over the following two years of counselling, Amelia was gradually able to piece together some form of Sarah's life, wondering, as her story unfolded, what traumatic events had taken place to turn a seemingly happy girl into the sad, lonely woman who stood before her on that first day.

Although Sarah found it hard to talk at first, painstakingly bit by bit, a picture was built-up and formed in Amelia's mind. Later, discovering more of the story from other sources, Amelia was able to make some sense of it.

Sarah first talked of her mum and dad in order to portray a sense of who they were. She began with her dad, James Whyte, as a young man, and as she spoke of him, she hesitated slightly.

"At this point Sarah paused when I detected a hint of regret in her voice, and wondered why? Not wishing to interrupt her train of thought however, I kept quiet and she continued."

James seemed to be a gentleman, in every sense of the word. Although mild-mannered, he was courageous, loving and by all accounts, quite outstanding. Sarah, of course, had not been born at this time in his life. She disclosed this earlier part of their lives, as it had been told to her by her parents.

Amelia found her story intriguing, sad, weirdly unusual, and downright unbelievable in parts – or was it? There actually seemed to be not one but three victims in the tale, each one a victim of different circumstances. Here she retells the story, as recorded in the file, mostly in Sarah's own words. Follow Sarah through her life, reading of her family and friends. Then, form your own opinion of Sarah's lot, to conclude what had ultimately brought her to such a sad state that she had no will to live.

CHAPTER TWO

It was October 1945 and James Whyte was on his way to enjoy a night out at the Beach ballroom in Aberdeen, Scotland. He felt out of his comfort zone to be wearing a suit and tie again after so long in uniform. While walking to the ballroom, he was reflecting, on the past six years of his life, having served his country as a soldier, in the second world war. He had been a gunner on the Bofor guns before training as a wireless operator. At the end of the war, he had been stationed in Berlin. This was in order to help the German people start to rebuild the devastation, which they too had suffered. He had gone to war as a young boy of eighteen and was now a man of twenty-four. He had faced danger, seen abhorrent atrocities and with the death of some of his comrades and friends, felt much sadness and pain. He had made a promise to himself not to think or talk about the war, but was now looking forward to more peaceful and happier times. He kept this promise for many years until the rawness of it all started to abate.

When he entered the ballroom his eyes set upon little Martha Fraser, who had been a neighbour of his, prior to going off to war. She had been a small, cheeky-faced, feisty girl with her hair always in plaits. Now he could see she had grown up quite a bit. Her chestnut brown hair, being held back at either side by a sparkly clip, hung loosely down her back and shimmered in the glow of the mirrored ballroom globe. She was small in stature but nicely proportioned. 'Hmm yes,' he thought to himself, she had grown into an attractive woman and he felt drawn to ask her up for a dance. Martha had said, "Yes," and they were just finishing off the dance when he asked if she would like some ice cream, this, being sold on the balcony of the dance hall. Trying to impress, he bought a very fancy concoction of different flavours not realising that she only liked vanilla. Martha, being the plain speaking person she was, told him straight she did not like fancy ice cream. He laughed, and liked her that bit more for her directness. They got chatting and enjoyed a good evening together

James asked if he could walk Martha home. As they strolled along on the grass beside the beach boulevard, he found that Martha had a fun-quirky streak. She said, "I bet you can't walk on your hands?" "I can", he replied and promptly got up on to his hands showing how fit he was by walking along on them. Martha quickly picked up the coins, which, had fallen from his pockets, and ran into the darkness, where she stood perfectly still with a grin on her face. At first, James was not sure which way she had gone, then, suddenly the moon came out from behind a dark sky and lit up her hiding place. He ran to catch her in his arms and they both laughed. Just for a few seconds they looked into each other's eyes. "I think I had better take you home now, it's getting late," he said. He walked Martha home but was a bit reluctant to take the friendship any further at that stage. He was well aware of the Fraser family and their stories. Martha was the baby of a family of eleven children and much adored by her siblings who fiercely protected her. He knew, he had much to overcome, in order to be accepted, by the Fraser clan. They were a well-known and much liked family in the area, even if a little coarse round the edges.

That night after dropping Martha home James lay in bed and thought of some of the stories he had heard about the Fraser family. Martha's dad, Aubrey, had been born and raised in Hull. His family owned a grocer's store, and, when his father owed money, they would up sticks and move under cover of darkness, to avoid payment, then, open a new shop elsewhere, sometimes under a different surname. This had happened a few times in his young life and finally, at the age of fourteen, Aubrey had decided to run away to sea from his unscrupulous and brutal father. A man who rendered out frequent beatings on his son leaving life-long scars on his back. The young Aubrey became a cabin boy and from then on loved the sea and anything connected with it, even though he endured hardships on board as a youngster. As a man, he became a skipper of a trawler and would go off to sea for long periods at a time in order to bring home a good catch of fish. It was a hard life in those days, for the fishermen, especially when the catch of fish was scant, and there was little money for their families.

One Christmas Aubrey had come back from sea with a particularly small catch, and after sharing out most of the money with the crew, this having been acquired through the sale of the fish, found there to be very little left for his own wife and family. Regina, his wife, was very upset, as she had nothing to give their family for Christmas. Regina and Aubrey had watched with sinking hearts, as their children hung up their stockings with much excitement, on Christmas eve. On Christmas morning however, the couple could not believe their eyes when they saw the miracle. There was something in each of the children's stockings. The truth was, of kindly neighbours getting together to help out the family, even though they had very little themselves. It was testament to how well liked the Fraser family were. For years to come when children announced their disbelief in Santa Claus, they were told the story of the Fraser family who had no money or presents for their children, but how, on Christmas morning, each child had a gift in their stocking from St Nick. This was a favourite story of the Fraser clan's future generations to help change the minds of any disbelievers in Santa.

Some of the other Fraser family stories handed down were of how Martha's second oldest sister, Nellie, was the first lady to swim from the river Dee to the river Don. She was a very accomplished swimmer, and had decided to dive from the Victoria Bridge and proceeded to do this swim for the hell of it. At the time, there had only been a few bystanders, however, sometime later, the event was documented in the newspaper, by her son.

One of the most poignant stories, which James remembered, was when Aubrey, with seven other men, including one of his sons, had gone trawl fishing on the Ocean Princess up to the Skerries. The Skerries is a group of rocky islets lying 3 kilometres offshore from Carmel Head at the northwest corner of Anglesey, Wales. Although this could be dangerous, Aubrey had been fishing there many times before and could navigate his way with great precision. However, on this particular day, the weather had turned stormy and the waves were getting higher. The crew were frantically bailing out the water but to no avail, therefore, Aubrey decided to send out a Mayday call to the owner of the Ocean Princess. After he had done so, an enormous wave crashed down on the fishing vessel, eliminating all power. The local newspaper managed to get a hold of this story and were quickly at Regina Fraser's door. She and her family were totally unaware of what had happened until then, when they spent the whole night worrying and wondering if the crew were alive or dead. The article in the newspaper had been sensationalised, by showing the heading, *'Father and son on board doomed vessel.'*

With heavy hearts, Aubrey and his crew had put on as much clothing as they could, in order to have a quicker death, when the time came to be gobbled up by the cruel sea. Aubrey decided to try one last desperate attempt to get some power from the boat and said a quick prayer. Suddenly, there was a spark of power from the boiler and he managed to get the trawler moving, albeit limping, into Lerwick harbour. There, the crew, were all treated for shock, except Aubrey. He had gone to the quietness of a graveyard where he had fallen to his knees and holding his head in his hands had sobbed, while at the same time giving thanks to God for saving both himself and his crew. He, was hailed as a hero

"Indeed, I do have a lot to live up to," James said to himself as he yawned and drifted off to sleep dreaming of Martha.

CHAPTER THREE

Young Martha had a beautiful voice and loved to sing. She had joined a concert party, *'Cocks O the North'*, and toured Aberdeenshire singing with them. She thoroughly enjoyed her time with the group and laughed, when she saw how the girls chased after Terry, the handsome piano player, who only had eyes for her. After a few years with the group, Martha had become engaged to Terry, some two months prior to dancing with James. Although only having been with James on the one occasion, she felt more of a connection to him than she had ever done for Terry and now knew marriage to him was out of the question. She decided to break off the engagement and leave the concert party. This was very hard for her to do but she did not wish to hurt Terry by staying with the musical group, while she was developing feelings for James. However, she would certainly miss singing with them. From then on, she only sang in her bath or at family get-togethers.

James had a musical bent also. His parents had paid for music lessons on the violin when he was a boy. As he got older he taught himself to play other instruments such as the mandolin, banjo and the accordion, the latter being his favourite. When he left school at 15 he went to work as an apprentice plumber and saved hard for 2 years so that he could buy himself an accordion. He took great care of it, lovingly returning it to its case when not in use. It was his pride and joy and James played it to perfection. When he joined the army, his parents gave him a squeezebox concertina to take with him in place of his precious accordion. He carried it with him always and would take it out to play a tune when either he or his comrades were at a low ebb. They loved to have a 'sing-song,' to his accompaniment, and it helped them through the gloomy days of World War 2.

James and Martha's friendship blossomed into love and they were married on the 27th of December 1948. The Fraser clan, seeing how happy James made their little Martha, were, only too pleased to welcome him into the family.

While on honeymoon, which they spent in Edinburgh in a bed and breakfast for a week, James finally had the last laugh on Martha. She had the habit of opening her Kirkby grips, for holding her hair, with her teeth, before sliding them into place. One morning, a Kirkby grip, became stuck between her teeth and would not budge. She was not amused, and had to walk, holding her hand over her mouth, to the chemist, where the offending clip was finally prised out. "Thank goodness for that," she cried, letting out a huge sigh of relief while James stood smirking.

The couple lived with James's parents being as there was more room to spare than in Marthas'. James's mother was a genteel, usually quiet-spoken lady, who, apart from her family, had two main passions in her life. These were the cinema and her precious little granddaughter Sarah, yet to be born. She loved to get dressed up and go to an afternoon showing at the cinema once a week then, come home and relate the whole film to the family, before starting supper. This she did, in her fully animated persona with her pale blue eyes twinkling and her whole body re-living the story from the film. This was the only time her voice would elevate a notch or two with excitement. James and Martha would listen and smile, but oh, how they wished she would re-live the tales in a shorter version when the hunger pangs began, especially when Martha became pregnant.

When little Sarah was born in March 1950 Martha decided, much as she loved her mother-in-law, to live with her own mum for a while to help take care of the baby so, the new family moved in with Regina and Aubrey as Martha's older siblings, were no longer living there. Sarah was a chubby baby with a head of thick red hair and endearing warm smile. She grew up encircled by a comfort blanket of love, fun, and laughter, within this large extended family

The Fraser clan were quite a noisy lot, especially when playing cards. This was their favourite pastime, when the whole family would get together. Their excitement growing into heated arguments during the play, with some of the family standing up and making accusations of cheating. Little Sarah found it quite frightening at times but they always made up and she would see that all was forgiven at the end of play when they showed their cheery smiles once again.

Her uncles, like her granddad Aubrey, also became skippers and mates, and it was the job of their wives to mend the torn nets and gut the fish, the *'Silver Darlings,'* as the Aberdonians called them. It was a hard life for them but to Sarah they always seemed happy. She was told lots of stories by her uncles about what happened at sea but wondered whether they were true or not, being as fishermen are known for telling *'tall tales.'*

The family picnic was the high spot of the summer. This, being when a bus was hired, to take them all to Nairn beach for the day. They would meet the bus at 6 am in the morning, but woe betide you if you were late, you literally missed the bus. Sarah used to get so excited about this special day with her fun loving family, there was nothing like it. Her dad forgot to set the clock alarm one year and they slept in and missed the trip. She was so upset and refused to speak to him for days afterwards. She always felt, that for some reason, which she could not understand, he did not really wish to be involved too much with her mother's side of the family and this saddened her.

During the day of these picnics, come rain or shine, Sarah would have such fun. She tried to outrun her cousins, aunts, and uncles, down the huge sand dunes, only to land up falling half way down and continuing rolling over, and over to the bottom, howling with laughter. There was always a superb picnic, sharing all the goodies the whole family had brought between them. Then there was the evening. . . .The bus would stop at a hotel pub on the way home for the adults to have a drink *(or two or three or four)*. As a child the memory of these evenings were weird to Sarah, the men would be swaying and spilling their drinks and she would laugh at the thought of two of her mum's sisters always singing, '*Sisters, sisters, there were never such devoted sisters,'* and all the rest of the song in their own inimitable way. They would sing their hearts out, always the same song every year. That song was in-grained in her memory together with the image they portrayed singing it while swaying from side to side with arms around each other. To Sarah, these were such happy days, and so fondly remembered.

Her uncle Timmy, her mum's youngest brother, was the joker in the family and was always kidding around with his nephews and nieces, who never knew what he would do next. His favourite trick was to pretend there was a dog behind them and point to it. As they turned, he would bark, throwing his voice in the manner of a ventriloquist across the room, thus, although hearing the bark, they could never find the dog. It was most bewildering to the children.

James's family was considerably smaller than Martha's. He had only one brother and sister. They were of a much more refined and quieter nature so he always found it hard to accept Martha's large noisy family and Sarah felt this continued all throughout her life, which affected the relationship between father and daughter. She could never understand why he did not love all these funny, eccentric people as much as she did. As he liked a quieter life, he tried, to some extent, to keep her from getting too involved with them. This irked Sarah somewhat, as she was always at her happiest, when being sociably surrounded, with lots of people, and never understood this side of her father.

There had been a lot of sadness in James's family. His father had worked in the shipyard where a cradle had come loose and shed its load over him damaging his back, thus making him disabled. He was never able to work again. James's brother had been a pilot, in WW2 and his plane had crashed. Although he was a survivor, he had been left a shadow of his former self. The accident had caused him brain damage, and he had also developed Parkingon's disease. Unfortunately, he had become a character, which Sarah, as a little girl, was rather afraid of. She especially disliked when he frequently asked her for, '*a cheeper.*' She often wondered where this word originated from but knew he meant a kiss. Thus, she actually grew up with an aversion to kissing, spoiling many a romantic moment in her future life. James found it hard to get close to his daughter because of the uneasiness around the Fraser family. This, was intensified by her aversion to being kissed. Thus, causing him great sadness, as the affection and love he had for Sarah, did not seem to be reciprocated by her.

Sarah's aunt Katherine, her dad's sister, was okay she thought, although her mum didn't seem to get on with her. Something had happened to upset Martha, it was highly mysterious and she was at a loss to understand the rift between these two family members, but felt she had to be loyal to her mum. She would avoid talking about her aunt in front of Martha. She also felt for her father, as she could see the upset it caused him. Her aunt Katherine, together with her husband and son and daughter, stayed with, and looked after her granddad Whyte in what had originally been her grandma and granddad Whyte's house.

Sarah had only been eighteen months old when her grandma Whyte started to drop things and then lose the use of her arms and legs. She was diagnosed, as having a muscle wasting disease, causing her death, six painful months later, when finally, the muscles in her throat rendered her incapable of speaking or eating. Motor Neuron Disease was a terrible death and not really understood in those days.

CHAPTER FOUR

By the time Sarah was two years old (the terrible 2s) James and Martha had a house of their own. Sarah was prone to speaking to strangers, wandering off and getting lost and being contrary. She was a cute little thing, with a beautiful smile, happy disposition and a lovely head of thick red hair. Martha found this hard to control with either ribbons or clips. Each time she tried to tame the mane, the hair adornments would simply bounce out again. The little girl was a tomboy and James and Martha had a worrying time with her. One day she walked down to the beach with an older friend and decided to take off her wee skirt and bury it in the sand. At the end of the afternoon, the skirt was nowhere to be found thus Sarah, dressed in only her pants and top walked home being stared at by passers-by. She cared not hoot, but her friend did!

On another day, while out in the park with her granddad Fraser she had wandered off, however, Aubrey had seen her and decided to say nothing but quietly follow his granddaughter, to see where she intended to go. Suddenly she turned round and said, "Oh there you are granddad." "Yes", he smiled, "here I am." When they got home, she proudly announced to her mum, "Granddad was lost but I found him." Aubrey thought her a funny wee thing but loved her dearly.

She loved playing with the local boys, and when her dad bought her a doll's pram for her fourth birthday, she decided to use it as a go-kart, down the lane beside the house, with her boyfriends. Needless-to-say, it did not keep in very good condition for long.

Getting all dressed up, was a pet hate for Sarah as a child, and one day when her mum had just finished attiring her in a new kilt for a relative's wedding, she asked if she could stand outside until they were all ready to go. Martha said, "Yes, but don't get dirty." Sarah, being Sarah, promptly decided to climb up on the fence and ripped the expensive garment much to her mother's dismay.

The most worrying account however, was when Sarah was over visiting her Grandad Whyte and, while the adults were chatting in the house, she was happily playing outside in the garden, or so they thought. The gate was always securely bolted shut, and the family usually had no worries about her getting out. On this particular day, she had worked away at the bolt for quite a while, loosening it until it slid open allowing her to escape through the gate. Then with no fear whatsoever, off she went out into the big wide world to explore. Because of her wanderings, James had taught her to say her address in case she ever got lost. A taxi was driving by and the driver could see the child was alone, so stopped the car and asked Sarah where she lived. When Sarah gave her address the man thought to himself, 'It's not possible for a little girl of this size to have wandered so far by herself.' He then decided to take her to a missing children's station down at the beach promenade. By this time, James and Martha had discovered their child was missing and were frantically searching when the taxi drove by with Sarah gleefully waving to them out of the window. They contacted the missing children's station to find she had indeed, been brought there. However, when they went to collect Sarah she threw a tantrum and refused to go with them as she was having such fun.

"Oh my God, this child will be the death of me!" Martha sighed, while trying to coax the struggling child away from the toys.

Her baby brother, William, was born when Sarah was four years old. When Martha came home with the baby, Sarah was adamant it was a girl whereupon, her mummy proceeded to show her his lower region and Sarah shrugged saying, "He might still change to a girl." She loved her baby brother very much but still hoped that one day he would become a girl and persisted in continually dressing him in her big doll's dresses and hats, which irritated Martha immensely. Her daughter certainly tried her patience.

CHAPTER FIVE

During the next year, before Sarah started school, she spent a lot of time with her granddad Fraser. This was to help Martha out because James was a plumber and as work was scarce, he often worked away from home. Most of the work was in the Queen's summer home at Balmoral, Birkhall estate on Royal Deeside, and the Queen Mother's home at Glamis Castle. While working at these Royal estates he felt privileged to have been able to talk to the Queen Mother and the very young Prince Charles and Princess Anne at times, while they were out playing in the gardens.

By this time, Aubrey had retired from the sea and now bred dogs, and Sarah would play with the puppies. He also owned a big black dog named Blackie, whom little Sarah adored and could be seen running alongside of him, up and down the back yard, laughing and skipping. She liked to try, being the operative word, and teach him tricks. Pointing her little fat index finger, while adopting her most strict stance, she would ask him to *'fetch the ball,'* which she had thrown across the yard seconds earlier. The dog would simply just stay put, gazing first at the ball then looking back at Sarah with puzzlement in his big dark eyes. She also tried to encourage him to give her his paw but again he would just simply look back at her. He just did not get it. Sarah would then bend down to chastise him, and he would smother her with wet soppy kisses. She could never stay annoyed with Blackie for long however, and would then wrap her arms around his neck nuzzling her face into his soft furry coat.

Now and then, as with all young children, Sarah would run a little too fast and trip over her feet in spectacular fashion. There would be a potent second's silence before her brain registered that she had hurt herself then, would come the ear-splitting siren of a long drawn out cry followed by tears. At that point, Blackie would lumber up to her and lick the tears from her cheeks. The cries would become whimpers, before stopping, and then, she would return to her old, happy self, again, thanks to her furry friend.

Passers-by seeing their antics, would laugh. This did not however, upset Sarah, she found she liked making people laugh, it made her feel good. Later in the day after one of these episodes, she was in the house with her mother and had been pondering with an idea. The four year old suddenly stood up straight, puffed out her chest and with hands on her hips announced to Martha, "I am going to be a clown when I grow up mummy." "Are you dear, that's nice," Martha said then chuckling would turn away from her daughter muttering to herself, "Over my dead body." Throughout her young life, Sarah, did not follow the career path of a clown, but every time she was laughed at, for doing silly things, she simply shrugged her shoulders, and laughed along with them, feeling better for it. From a young age, she appeared to have a good outlook on life.

Sarah's granddad would take her to the harbour, where he would meet up with his cronies, and watch, while the fresh fish was unloaded from the boats in order to be sold. She loved to listen to the chatter of the fishermen, while they set up their boxes of fish ready to be bought. Mesmerized, she would watch the old men scraping pieces from the tobacco blocks with their penknives and stuff it into their pipes. She was full of wonderment when they slipped the pipes in at the side of their mouths. Sucking in and puffing out, while at the same time, after striking their matches, trying to light up. After which, she would enjoy the smell of the tobacco as the wisps of smoke rose from the pipe bowls. This smell she never forgot, and in years to come, it always reminded her of the happy days spent with her loving granddad.

Her granddad used to coach her in spelling. Some days he would ask her to spell a few words, his favourites were, 'scissors' and 'machine.' Sarah loved to act and sing and as a reward, if she got them right, he would settle in his favourite chair, smoking his pipe beside the fire in the big black range, then he would let the little girl put on her show as only she knew how. Most of the songs she had learned from Martha. No one could sing as sweetly as her mummy she thought, and a contented grin would cross her face when Martha burst into song while having a bath or, in the more modern times of later years, a shower.

For the next year, prior to starting school, Sarah continued with her stubborn nature, when she did her best pouting, but even with her contrary ways, Aubrey and his granddaughter had a special bond and he always knew how to extract the best out of her.

CHAPTER SIX

At the age of five Sarah had to sit a wee test for entry to school. She was instructed to draw a house, but, in her contrary mind, she had decided she wanted to draw a rocket so, this is what she did. Her parents received the report that perhaps she may have some learning difficulty, but they knew better! They despaired of her and Martha gave out an exasperated laugh while thinking, 'Even 'though we used protection during intercourse, she still managed to get through.' Once she started school however, she seemed to settle down and announced to everyone, in no uncertain terms, "There is no-one like my teacher, she is always right."

The first year at her school was enjoyable for Sarah and all went well, but then her family moved house to another area where she had to start learning afresh at a new school. The headmaster took a dislike to Sarah and so seemed to take her to task for silly little things, like pulling leaves from hedges on the way home from school. Thus, primary school years were not particularly happy for her. While away from school however, she very much enjoyed trying to raise money for charity. She would put on little shows behind her house, hanging up an old curtain between the two large pillars down at the back of the house, in order to make a stage. Her friends then came and paid an old penny to watch Sarah singing. Their seats were on four stone steps leading up to the green, where washing was hung out to dry.

During the long summer holidays, she would organise jumble sales. Martha would sigh when she saw all the collected items lying in her veranda, ready to be, arranged for the sales, but at the same time feeling proud of her little girl's caring nature at such a young age. Sarah would diligently collect all the money from her shows and jumble sales until she had amassed enough to give to charity.

At the age of six, Sarah started going to the ABC Minor show at one of the cinemas on a Saturday morning with three of her cousins. Vince, Frankie and Kate were a few years older and into rock 'n roll. The show would start with cartoons and then an interval and finish with an instalment of an exciting hero film such as Zorro, the story of which, would be continued the following week. At the interval, rock and roll music was played, and the older boys and girls, in the audience, were invited on to the stage, in front of the big screen, for a dance session. Thrills and excitement shot through Sarah as she watched her cousins dancing. Vince would hold one of the girls on each side, where they would swivel on the balls of their feet, whilst flicking their wrists to the beat of the music, their skirts swirling from side to side around them. Holding their arms he would throw the girls, one at a time, over his back whilst they flipped up their legs then he would twist them round his hips, their long ponytails swishing around with the motion. Finally, he would throw each girl in turn to the ground, while keeping a grip on their arms, then slide them through between his legs before continuing to dance the threesome. They exhibited such high energy, while the dance was carried out extremely fast and furious. She thought they were fantastic dancers and wished she too could join in. *'Perhaps, some day when I am older, and with more practice,'* she thought. This dream was never realised, however, as by the time she had reached her sixteenth birthday, it was the mid-60s, and the rock n roll craze was overtaken by the emergence of a whole new dance craze.

She also had a fascination for the monitors who, with their torches, walked about the cinema building in the darkness, showing the children to their seats, and wanted so much to be one of them. By the time she was eleven years old, and her cousins had long stopped going to the ABC club, she had in fact become a monitor, which she enjoyed for a few months until she felt too old and found a new hobby in her life, '*Boys.*' The time had finally come for her to stop being a tomboy as she started to enjoy getting dressed up and showing more of her feminine side.

When Sarah reached eight years old, her granddad Fraser died and it shook her world. Then six months later her grandma Fraser also died of breast cancer. She could see the hurt and pain Martha felt at that time and thought about how she too would feel if she lost her parents. Being so young, however, she dismissed it as unthinkable at her age. She felt her mum would always be there, but still harboured a bit of a divide between herself and her dad.

Sarah began to accept that her brother was not going to change into a sister, and through the primary years, they grew closer. William was always clowning around, and also, very good at mimicking people, he really made her laugh. They both went to piano lessons and although Sarah didn't much take to it, William excelled. In the following years, he also went on to learn the guitar, after which he would get together with his university buddies, when they would all enjoy jamming sessions. Although William was quite a comedian, he had a serious side and from an early age wanted to be an architect. Martha used to, jokingly say of her children, "One has beauty and the other has brains," which irked Sarah somewhat.

The last year at primary school for Sarah should have been an exceptionally studious one, taking in as much educational knowledge as possible prior to the 11-plus exam. It was important for the young children to do their best in this exam, in order to ensure the prospect of further learning at senior secondary school, adding to the prospect of a decent working career in the future if they passed. It was, therefore, good to have the best teacher at this particular time. Unfortunately, in her last year at primary school, Sarah's teacher, Miss Clements, who, being diagnosed with stomach cancer, was off for most of this important period of time, the disease finally claiming her life. The replacement teacher was not adequately experienced, therefore, none of her class passed this crucial exam. They were missing Miss Clements dreadfully, and unfortunately, for all the children in her class, the momentum of her teachings, had been cut short.

Life went on for the brother and sister much like any other siblings, having their fights along the way. However, by the time Sarah was at secondary school, Martha was working, so although Sarah did love her brother, she resented having to watch him during the school holidays when she would have preferred to go out with her friends.

Martha, although small in height, was the boss of the household. She was a good wife and brilliant mother who could sometimes be strict but was very fair, and much loved by her children. She had brought them up to learn respect for what was right and the one thing she would not tolerate within her family was the telling of lies.

Sarah could not remember ever having to be physically taken to task by her mother except once. At the age of eleven she, and her three friends, were now starting to play with, and take notice of the opposite sex. One day, she and some of her friends had been playing a game of hide and seek, partnering up with some of the neighbourhood boys. They were spotted hiding in the long grass around the woods beside their flats and just typically fooling around as youngsters do. Unbeknown to her, a nosey neighbour had told Martha of the youngsters' escapades, sneering and exaggerating their exploits. When getting home Martha confronted Sarah asking her rather abruptly, "What have you been doing today?" Hearing the tone of her mother's voice, Sarah suddenly felt guilty about lying in the grass with the boys so answered, "I have been round at my friend's house all afternoon." Martha's mood totally changed, her face contorted and turned red as she proceeded to shout, "You are telling lies, Mrs McMann saw you all lying in the long grass." She then took hold of her daughter's arm and smacking her bottom threw her across the room banging her arm against the wall. Sarah slowly got up feeling shocked, battered and dazed. Rubbing at her bruised arm, she then apologised to Martha, learning a very valuable lesson that day. It does not pay to lie, and from that day forward, she always tried to be truthful.

CHAPTER SEVEN

During the summer break of 1962, just prior to starting secondary school, a new girl moved into the neighbourhood. Lizzie was a thin slightly poker-faced girl with mousey brown, medium length hair. This, she fashioned to be held to one side, with a clip and would gently bounce as she walked. She was not particularly striking but oozed charm and charisma, allowing her to manipulate those around her. Everyone, when in her presence, felt this, including Sarah. Lizzie was the offspring of a single parent whose father had left when she was a baby. This girl lived an entirely different family life to Sarah with only her mother, who worked two jobs to make ends meet. Sarah found her to be good fun with a wicked sense of humour, and they became friends.

Sarah was now twelve years old and had started secondary school along with Lizzie. She had been a bit apprehensive on hearing rumours that some of the pupils were real live wires and would get up to all sorts of mischief, especially the boys. This, was clarified while attending for choir practice one day. Some of the boys, having arrived there early, seemed to have hatched a plan to torment the choir teacher. Before he arrived, they knocked out the seat of the wicker chair and inserted the large open wickerwork waste paper basket. Next, they lifted the long wooden desk, which served as the schoolmaster's table, and turned it around. There were two drawers on one side in which the dreaded strap, (or the 'Tawse' as it was called), was kept for errant schoolchildren. When Mr Kimble (the music teacher), a small bald-headed man with glasses, arrived and tried to sit down, his bottom slid into the waste paper basket. He jumped up shouting, "Whose handiwork is this?" at the class. Then, reached for the drawer to take out the strap. Realising the drawer was not where it should be his anger rose. His face shone crimson and the veins stood up throbbing on his forehead. Sarah thought he might have a heart attack and felt sorry for Mr Kimble at the time, but did laugh about it after. Needless-to-say, the boys, who were known to be the usual troublemakers, were wheedled out and sent to the headmaster's room for punishment. She also witnessed other such incidents throughout her first year at secondary school. It was like scenes from the St Trinians films, only with boys instead of girls.

During June, on the school sports day, Sarah had slipped whilst carrying some equipment from the gym to the playing fields. A hand was extended out to help her up. There stood a fair-haired young boy with strikingly green eyes. "Are you okay?" he asked. Sarah jumped up feeling embarrassed, and answered in an abrupt voice, "I'm fine." "Okay," he said and went on his way. She watched him as he walked away and thought how tall and athletic he looked in his shorts and T-shirt. Later she discovered that the boy's name was Darren and he was exceptionally good at sports, winning most of the school trophies and in fact was the school captain. However, he was due to leave school at the end of term. 'Oh well,' she thought, 'he's too old for me anyway.'

At this time, Lizzie also got together with a boy whose name was Ryan. Ryan had a rather inflated opinion of himself and tended to put Lizzie down. They had slept together and he appeared to use her and drop her whenever he wished. However, Lizzie was smitten, and appeared to be under his control.

A week after the sports day incident, Sarah was on her way home from school with Lizzie. Darren was walking past when he recognised her and asked how she was after her fall. She replied that she was ok and thanked him for asking. They then got talking, and for the next few days, each time Sarah was walking home from school, Darren would join her. Eventually they became a couple. Darren started to come round to Sarah's house some evenings, after homework of course, and they would stand under the archway, adjacent to her house, talking and cuddling until Martha called her in. A year later Darren had left school and was now working as a television engineer in the same company as his father. He asked Sarah to go with him to his annual works Christmas dance and although she was only 13, and still at school, her mum allowed her to go as, Darren's parents would also be accompanying the couple. Sarah was so excited as Martha had bought her a lovely dress which was fitted in at the waist with a bow then fluted out with a number of stiff petticoats. The outfit was finished off adding her first pair of grown up shoes with low heels. On the evening of the dance, a taxi, in which Darren and his parents had arrived, stopped at her door to pick her up, whereupon, she was given instructions, to be home by eleven thirty.

The dance had been an enjoyable experience but left Sarah feeling rather immature and out of her depth with Darren's work colleagues. Although she liked Darren very much she decided he was too old for her and let him down gently. He was quite upset but reluctantly accepted her decision. Although they vowed to remain friends, their worlds were now completely separate thus giving no reason to see one another again. So ended, her first love.

CHAPTER EIGHT

In May 1964, when Sarah had just turned fourteen, the newspapers reported two cases of typhoid fever in the city of Aberdeen. The typhoid outbreak became widely known. Each day reports were made of more cases, and the people of Aberdeen were very fearful of catching the disease. There were over 400 cases altogether. The City hospital, was especially quarantined, to take care of the typhoid cases. The staff there were having difficulty coping with the large numbers who had fallen ill. Other hospitals were therefore, forced to take the overspill. Crazy rumours spread of deaths and bodies lying at the beach area still to be disposed of. Some establishments closed down, including schools, to help stop the spread of the disease. Rules of strict hygiene, for all to follow, were set out. The whole situation was becoming extremely frightening and Martha and James, along with all the other citizens of Aberdeen, feared for their families.

The tenpin bowling club remained open and Sarah, together with her brother, met in with Lizzie and her friends there most days. However, they did adhere to the hygiene laws of no sharing of food or drink, and washing their hands thoroughly, especially after a visit to the loo. Thankfully, none of Sarah's relatives or friends were among those who had contracted typhoid. After twenty-eight days, there were no more cases. Shortly thereafter, the formal public statement, giving the 'all clear', was announced. It was the news, which all the citizens of Aberdeen had been anxious to hear. Everyone had survived and there were actually no deaths. According to scientific evidence, Argentinean corned beef had been the source of the causative organism. All the people of Aberdeen had certainly learned the importance of hygiene during that time.

The year after the typhoid outbreak, James came home to an empty house to find a note on the kitchen table. He read that Martha and his daughter were both out with friends and William was at the library studying for school exams. William still wished very much to become an architect, and was studying hard, in order to go to the Robert Gordon school, and hopefully, do well enough, to be accepted thereafter, for the Scott Sutherland School of Architecture.

James had had a particularly tiring day and slumped down into his favourite armchair. His thoughts drifted to work. He now worked for the town and in his capacity of City Building Inspector, he had noticed a big change in public hygiene. The city was much cleaner, toilets were spotless, and there was always soap, hot water and toilet paper in all of the establishments, including the public toilets. Aberdonians were still known to wash their hands after going to the loo, more than anywhere else in the country. On this thought, the tiredness left his body and he smiled with pride when he thought of how hard the people, living in Aberdeen, worked to keep the city clean.

While at secondary school, Sarah worked at the weekends in a rather posh restaurant on Bridge Street, alternating between waitressing and serving behind the tea bar. She did not particularly enjoy working in this establishment, as, although everything looked good to the customers, behind the scenes it was quite different. The manageress was a stiff, serious faced individual who treated her staff with uncaring expletives. Also, Sarah did not care for the greasy cooking smell, which still seemed to cling around her hair and hands, when going out on a Saturday evening with her friends, even after vigorously showering.

One Saturday morning the manageress had just finished creating a large plate of petite patterned rolls of butter, ready to put in the refrigerator for hardening, prior to being set out on the tables for the customers. However, she had inadvertently left it lying on the counter where one of Sarah's colleagues was working behind the tea bar. The colleague had accidently knocked some glasses off an overhanging shelf, and they had smashed to the ground sending a spray of small shards of glass around the tea bar. The colleague swept up the glass and tried to be thorough in cleaning the area. Later that day however, a customer complained of finding a small shard of glass in the butter, and the fault, should have been, placed firmly at the door of the manageress for leaving the balls of butter out of the fridge. However, she denied all knowledge, and the girl who had dropped the glasses, was instantly fired. Sarah, who had witnessed it all, could not believe the situation, and felt so sorry for her colleague. This was the final straw, she made up her mind, she, was not going to work under these conditions anymore therefore, left at the end of her shift, relieved not to have to return to that dreadful place the following weekend.

Lizzie and Sarah started again to go tenpin bowling with other friends and they teamed up with some boys from school, one of these being Ryan. They all started to see each other more frequently, and pairing off as boyfriends and girlfriends, they would meet at the tenpin bowling or go to the cinema. Lizzie had a sometimes, turbulent friendship with Sarah. Although she did want to have her as a friend, she was jealous of her. There were times when Sarah would not feel right about things Lizzie made her do but she so desperately wanted to keep her friendship and would do practically anything to please her. She recalled the time Lizzie decided her breasts were too small and asked Sarah to rub them daily, as this would make them larger and she, in turn, would do the same to Sarah. Sarah felt a bit shocked, but in order to please her friend, thought she would 'give it a try'. Each day, at Lizzie's house, she tentatively cupped Lizzie's small mounds in her hands and gently massaged them for a few minutes and then Lizzie returned the favour. She felt a sort of naughtiness while doing this however, was quite relieved when Lizzie dropped this rather absurd idea a few weeks later.

Although Lizzie was normally a good friend to Sarah, she was more than a little jealous of the love shown by James and Martha to their daughter and her dark side would sometimes get the better of her. During these times, she would mentally hurt Sarah. At the beginning of one of the summer breaks from school the two girls had argued, this, having been, precipitated by Lizzie. After this, she had then turned all their friends against Sarah throughout the following six weeks of their school holidays. At this time she was happy to see Sarah feeling very lonely for the first time in her life and it was a feeling Sarah did not like one bit. This was just one of the spiteful episodes metered out by Lizzie. Sarah eventually apologised rather pathetically to Lizzie in order to feel accepted by her again. Unfortunately, this was the future trend in order for Sarah to keep Lizzie's friendship. Sarah did secretly get some satisfaction of revenge however, when she saw how upset Lizzie got when being dropped by Ryan. Once, she even went out with him a few times, hoping to upset Lizzie even more. It was not really in her nature to be cruel, and feeling very guilty about this situation, she decided to finish the short relationship she'd had with Ryan. When Martha heard about these revengeful episodes by Lizzie, she comforted her daughter and said, "Just remember that the birds always peck at the best fruit." Martha apparently liked her quotes.

In their last year at school, Lizzie tried her best to stop Sarah studying for the exams. She put pressure on her and called her a 'geek' and 'nerd' along with other derogatory names to belittle her. This was yet another attempt to put Sarah down and make sure she would not do well.

At the weekends, when her mother stayed over at a friend, Lizzie would have the flat to herself. One weekend she asked, Michael, one of Ryan's friends, back to the flat, along with Sarah and Ryan. By this time, Lizzie and Ryan had been having sexual relations frequently and Lizzie had told Sarah how wonderful it was, trying to goad her into doing the same. Although Sarah would do many things for Lizzie, she was not ready, at that time, to be sexually active and walked out

As she arrived home early on the Saturday evening from Lizzie's flat, she heard James and Martha discussing her granddad Whyte's will. He had died a few weeks earlier after some years of illness and disablement. "My sister took great care of and looked after dad for a long time, she deserved to have everything left to her," she heard James say, to which Martha replied rather too loudly, "She persuaded him to leave all his money and the house to her. He left a considerable amount of money as well as the house and by leaving it to Katherine, it will ultimately go to her children. Your dad had four grandchildren, two of which being yours, and they should have received something from their granddad. It's your children who have missed out." Sarah crept back out quietly and took a walk to think about this revelation, now realising why her mother did not care much for her aunt. She decided that she agreed with her dad in, that her aunt had taken great care of her granddad, for a few years, and did deserve, to be left everything for her efforts. At that stage in her young life, the money did not seem important, and she decided to reassure her mum of this if it came up in conversation in the future.

When she attended school on the following Monday, she was absolutely distraught to find that Lizzie had spread a story of how she had acted provocatively towards Michael and then, while teasing him, had brushed him off at the last moment. She could not understand why a so-called friend could spread such lies about her and it was at this point she gave serious consideration as to whether or not to continue their friendship.

It was near the end of term and the final school dance was looming. Being popular, three boys had asked Sarah to the dance, but she really wanted to go with Kevin. He was a bit of a rough diamond with a cheeky smile and good sense of humour. Even though he smoked, which was one of Sarah's dislikes, she still felt attracted to him. He, was very laid back and had quite a few girls in tow, perhaps that was the attraction, and as he had asked her to the dance, she accepted. It turned out however, to be a bit of a disappointing night. Kevin did not pay her enough attention but was flirting with one of the other girls. They went out once or twice together after that, but it was clear to Sarah that he was not that interested in her, so she ended it and chalked it up to experience. Kevin knew Darren through playing football and left Sarah with the words ringing in her ears, 'You, should go back to Darren as, you were both good together.' She had brushed this aside at that moment but from time to time would think of Darren and wonder about Kevin's words.

After leaving school at the age of fifteen, Sarah passed the entrance exam for the Aberdeen College of Commerce to study secretarial subjects. Whilst there she met a new circle of friends, and only saw Lizzie on the odd occasion.

She now studied hard but still went out socialising and dated a couple of boys although there was nothing serious in the relationships. While travelling to college on the bus one day, a young man sat beside her. "Hello Sarah," he said, "how are you?" Surprised to hear her name, she turned her head and there saw Darren. She was pleased to see him and they immediately started talking, catching up. It turned out, the building of the company he worked for, was situated, on the same street as the college. They saw each other travelling on the bus quite often after that and Sarah enjoyed their chats. After a few meetings on the bus, Darren asked if she would like to go out with him and Sarah remembered Kevin's words, *'Why not give it another try,'* she thought. However, after having gone out on a couple of dates, she felt there was no spark between them and now knew she only wanted to be friends. When she finished her two years at college, there was no more bus travel. Her chats with Darren ceased thus closing another chapter of her life.

CHAPTER NINE

Her first full time position was with a company who eradicated pests such as insects and rodents. The company had two divisions, Pest Control and Woodworm/Dry Rot, each headed by a manager. Sarah, was employed as secretary, to Pest Control, and the secretary to Woodworm/Dry Rot, was Rosie, one of the girls from her class at college, but not one she had known well. Sarah enjoyed her job and got to know Rosie better over chats at quiet times and tea breaks, whereupon a good friendship formed between the two young girls. During this time, she also attended evening classes to obtain a higher certificate in shorthand, to better her career.

Sarah's teenage years were during the 'swinging sixties' with mini and midi fashion, free love and the Pill. She loved the flower power fashion with chiffon dresses at just above the knee in length, and the wearing of flowers in her hair.

On a Sunday evening in early May 1967, when Sarah was not in any relationship and Lizzie and Ryan had broken up, yet again, the two girls decided to go dancing. Sarah had now grown into a very attractive young woman with her long red hair, dark blue eyes, a slightly curvy figure, beautiful smile, and the most dazzling perfectly formed white teeth. When she smiled, hearts melted. Even as a little girl her aunts and uncles would remark how pretty she was, and, as an adult, friends and colleagues remarked how lovely she was, both in looks and nature. Although she thought it nice of them to say so, it embarrassed her, and the irony was that although Sarah outwardly appeared self-confident she told me she never really felt that way about herself.

The two girls were excitable and chatty while getting dressed in their brightly coloured, chiffon, dresses, with a flower attached carefully in position to one side of each of their respective heads. The dance hall was the same one where, some years prior, James and Martha had first danced but not, of course, sporting the same fashion.

After a somewhat boring evening, two young men approached and asked the girls up for the last dance. While up dancing, Sarah had some quick looks at her partner. He was of medium height and had jet-black hair, swept back at the sides with a fringe, falling forward onto his forehead. His face, having been tanned by the sun, was rather striking against his light-coloured shirt and dark jacket. He had an Italian look about him and she thought him rather dishy.

When the dance finished the two friends thanked the boys and went to collect their coats from the cloakroom. "Do you know if they are seeing us home?" Lizzie asked. "I don't know, they didn't ask," replied Sarah. When they emerged from the cloakroom, the two young men took hold of the girls' hands with the presumption of seeing them home. Sarah thought that the height of rudeness but went along with it anyway. When they arrived at their houses, the two girls said their good nights to one another, then went their separate ways. The young man accompanied Sarah to her door and introduced himself as Fraser. "Oh, what a coincidence that's my mother's maiden name," she smiled, and softening towards him, talked a while. He asked if Sarah would go out with him the following week and they arranged a meeting place outside the large Saxons shoe shop in the city centre at 7 pm on the following Tuesday.

When the evening of the date arrived, Sarah got herself ready and took the bus into town. Not feeling too confident in herself, she really did not expect him to turn up. She arrived at the large glass-fronted building at exactly 7 pm and went quite a bit inside to look at the shoes in the arcade windows. After waiting for fifteen minutes, and deciding she had been 'stood up', she walked out from the arcade intending to go home. Hearing a toot on a car horn, she turned and there, a few yards from the shop, was Fraser. He had not seen her enter the shop arcade and she had not been looking for a car so they had both been wasting time waiting for one another. She felt pleased and excited to see him there. They decided to go and see the film, 'The Family Way,' starring Hayley Mills and Hywel Bennet, two of Sarah's favourite stars at the time, then, as it turned out to be a lovely sunny evening, went on to a touring fair which was only in Aberdeen for a week.

They had both really enjoyed the evening, and Sarah saw a whole, different side, to Fraser. He was handsome, funny, thoughtful and interesting. He spoke so well she held her breath at times lest she might miss a word he said. When they said goodnight he gave Sarah a quick kiss, softly brushing her lips, and asked to see her again. Feelings, she had never experienced before, stirred within her, and she could not wait for the next date. That night she fell asleep, with her mind playing over the evening, and thinking of how, for the first time in her life, she had actually enjoyed a kiss.

After this first night, they started going out regularly, especially enjoying their nights out dancing at the Beach Ballroom. The song most played was 'Unchained Melody' by the Righteous Brothers and this was to become 'their song.' It was, re-released again in 1990, thanks to its use in the movie 'Ghost.' Fraser's pet name for Sarah was 'Cuddles.' Sarah loved when he put his arm around her and whispered this seductively in her ear. He also used it within his long, loving, letters to her, while away on business courses. She enjoyed receiving his letters, of which there were three in total, and thought his handwriting was very articulate and neat. However, she missed him desperately when he was away. The letters were carefully stored in a drawer, and re-read at her leisure.

One evening Lizzie happened to bump into Fraser on her way home. She started to flirt with him and said he would be better off going out with her, being as Sarah was very spoiled and would only end up making him unhappy. Once again, she was trying to hurt Sarah. Fraser, however, was having none of it. He was falling for Sarah in a big way, and thought her to be the most kind-natured, loving and beautiful young woman he had ever known. Thankfully, this time, Lizzie's charm had not worked.

Sarah thought life could not get any better. She thoroughly enjoyed the company she was working with, and got to know Rosie very well over their little chats. Rosie was a tall young woman with quite a curvaceous figure, long straight glossy black hair, a twinkle in her eyes, and a cheery smile. She struck Sarah as a very caring person, and learned that her mum had fostered quite a number of children in her life. *What a wonderful woman she must be,'* thought Sarah. She did get to meet Rosie's mum a little later and could see the resemblance between mother and daughter, both had the same twinkly eyes, which always gave the appearance of a warm cheery smile. Sarah enjoyed talking to Rosie and felt she could confide anything in her. The two woman became firm friends. When Rosie met Rob Black, while out at a club one weekend, and started meeting him regularly, she would enjoy recalling details of the meetings to Sarah who in turn, did the same of her evenings out with Fraser.

Dates out with Fraser were great fun. When they kissed, she loved the feel of his thick soft lips on hers. After two months, she craved more. She wore lower provocative necklines and, once or twice, a dress with a zip on the front pulled down as low as she dare, showing some cleavage, hoping to lure him into caressing her body. He seemed to resist for quite a while then one evening, while kissing her, after seeing her home, he slipped his hand inside her bra. A tingle shot through Sarah, and, she blew out a sharp gasp as his hand gently cupped and caressed her breast. This was much better than the experience she'd had, as a young girl, with Lizzie. She instinctively pressed up against him while kissing, enjoying the experience, albeit through their clothes. Each time they met, the feelings were running high, and Sarah felt as if she would burst with excitement at his touch. One evening, standing in the lobby downstairs from her parents flat, after a night out, she started to unzip his trousers and caress his member, loving the feeling of making him erect to the point of ejaculation, but they held back from full sexual penetration for fear of Sarah becoming pregnant. She had only just turned seventeen and knew this would be disastrous however much she wanted more.

Christmas was a favourite time of year for Sarah and that first Christmas together was very memorable. Christmas Eve was so very magical to her. Fraser picked her up at 7.30 pm in his dad's car, and after a candlelit meal at a restaurant (this being a new craze during the end of the 1960s), they decided to go to the late night service at her local church. They emerged at five minutes past midnight, to find snowflakes quietly falling, forming a thin white covering on the ground. The trees, surrounding the church, sparkled in the beams of light emanating from the surrounding street lamps while the candles flickered in the church windows. It was certainly beautiful and Sarah thought it a perfect Christmas card setting. She twirled around throwing her hands in the air and smiling happily as the flakes fell on her hair and eyelashes. "Merry Christmas Cuddles," Fraser laughed, as he steadied her from toppling over, "And Merry Christmas to you too," Sarah replied. When they arrived at her house, Fraser gave her a present to open. She squealed with delight when she opened the gift to find a leather bound five-year diary with a key to lock away its secrets, and over the next few years, she loved committing all her special moments within its pages, knowing it was for her eyes only.

On that first Hogmanay, Sarah and Fraser stayed overnight at his family home. His parents, being out of town for a few days, had left it at their son's disposal. They spent a romantic evening together enjoying having the empty house to themselves. Although they had planned to sleep in the same bedroom, they had separate beds. Through the night however, Sarah had felt cold, so Fraser came into her bed to help heat her up. He lay at her back with his arms around her. She was aware of his hard manhood at her back and she too became aroused. She turned to face him, burrowing into his chest and inhaling his scent. She then took hold of his hand and put it on her breast under her nightie. "Oh God Sarah," he gasped, lifting the garment over her head then dropping it onto the floor. "You are so beautiful." She tugged at the underpants he was wearing, pulling them down, while kissing him passionately. At first they were urgent and hungry for each other, his hands were caressing her breasts then moving down to touch her clitoris whereupon she felt herself become very wet. She had now past the point of no return. "I'm a virgin Fraser," she whispered with a quiver in her voice. In a voice taken over with barely controllable emotion he replied, "I'll be gentle." His caresses became more tender, and Sarah, was swept into a sea, of unbelievable passion, such as she had never experienced before. As they held each other close in all their nakedness, she did not know which part of her body she wanted to feel nearest to him. Her heart was beating like a symphony, as their breathing became more heavy, and their feelings grew more out of control. Finally, Fraser entered her and their two bodies writhed together as one. Sarah's excitement grew to a point that she felt she could not breathe, and, as they both climaxed, she passed out. Fraser's voice was calling her name as she slowly came too. The intensity had been so strong she had fainted for a few minutes but she awakened exhilarated. "I didn't realise it could be so wonderful," she said, and now understood what Lizzie had meant when she had tried to describe the feelings of intercourse all those months ago.

Now that they had made love, they both wanted it more and more, and were intimate many times following this. They had sex while lying out in a field of corn in the warm sunshine. In a rowing boat out on a lake. Up against trees in the woods secluded from everything. Standing against a wall inside a derelict building. Also once when her parents were out, lying on Sarah's bed with her hair dripping wet after washing, the feelings of passion being too overpowering to wait until her hair had dried. In fact, any time and any place they could be intimate, each time more wonderful than the last. All of these steamy, passionate, love trysts, were recorded in Sarah's diary, to be relived through her eyes only, as she read and re-read them. She loved this man so much and wholeheartedly believed that he felt the same.

Six months into the relationship Sarah said how surprised she was that they had been going out for this length of time and had never had a cross word. However, what Sarah did not know, was that he was a jealous and possessive man and some arguments started shortly after that. He complained about the type of clothes she wore, changing her hairstyle and the shortness of her skirts. Sarah did not like this development. No one was going to tell her what to do so she decided to stop seeing him. However, it left her very unhappy and she missed him immensely.

A couple of weeks later, she was walking for her bus home, after her evening class, when it started to snow. Unbeknown to her, Fraser had been watching for the opportunity of getting her back. Suddenly, out of nowhere, he appeared in front of her, pretending to be meeting a friend for a drink in town. She was actually pleased to see him and he asked how she was. He was wearing a black duffle coat with the hood up. As she answered, she looked at his boyish smile and saw that the front of his hair was wet and falling over his face. This was a particular trait, which always tickled her fancy. A snowflake fell onto one of his eyelashes and she instinctively wiped it off with her finger. He pulled her close, kissed her, and in that special moment, she was once again, bewitched by him.

CHAPTER TEN

One day Rosie asked Sarah to meet her after work for a drink, in order to talk privately with her. Sarah said, "Of course," and wondered all day what this was about. She was totally, taken by surprise, when listening carefully to what Rosie related to her. Apparently, two months previously, on only one occasion, she and Rob had become rather intimate and although full penetration had not taken place, she had now found herself pregnant. They had decided to get married in three months' time, and hoped that Rosie's condition would not be too obvious then. Rosie confessed to Sarah that she was full of doubts, as, although she did think she loved Rob, she was not sure how married life would be for them. Rob was an only child whose birth mother had collapsed and died at a young age, in Union Street, from a brain haemorrhage when he was only a few months old. His father had remarried some years later, and Rob's stepmother could not have children of her own, so was rather possessive of him. No woman was good enough for her stepson. "She doesn't like me and thinks I have trapped her boy into marrying me, so, I'm afraid the marriage is doomed before it has started," Rosie said tearfully. Sarah put on her counselling hat, and while putting an arm around her friend, tried her best to comfort Rosie saying, "Everything will turn out alright, especially when Rob's stepmother sees her beautiful grandchild." Although Sarah left Rosie in happier spirits, that evening, she herself, felt some uncertainty about her friend's future.

While on her way home, she thought how unlucky Rosie had been to have found herself pregnant after only one night of passion. While thinking how fortunate, she had been, not to have found herself in the same position after having so many unprotected nights of pleasure with Fraser. Four months after her marriage Rosie gave birth to a daughter. The couple were delighted and named her Christina.

At the beginning of 1969, Sarah changed jobs and started work in the Assistant Matron's office within the Aberdeen Royal Infirmary. This was an extremely busy job, compared to where she had worked previously, but Sarah immersed herself into the work and thoroughly enjoyed the challenge of the new position.

During this time, and for the next eight years, she and Rosie lost touch. Lizzie had married Ryan and moved to England. Prior to the move Sarah had noticed Lizzie seemed much happier in herself, so was pleased for her one time friend, but made up her mind not to keep in touch or see her again. She knew nothing of the conversation that had taken place between Lizzie and Fraser a few years earlier. He had decided it was over and done with, and bringing it up would only upset her. Lizzie had previously confided to Sarah that it was her wish to have a family when she married but not before. She'd had a few scares when her monthlies were late in her teenage years, whilst, sleeping with Ryan. Therefore, Sarah felt it a sad irony, when meeting Lizzie's mother a couple of years after the marriage, and discovering that her old friend would never be able to conceive.

Fraser and Sarah were lucky enough to get a mortgage through Fraser's company at a low rate of repayment and bought their own little flat a year before the wedding. One morning, at the beginning of July 1970, Sarah was vomiting and did not feel well. A few days later she realised she had missed her period and as she was always regular, the realisation hit her that she might be pregnant. To her dismay, this was indeed, confirmed, six weeks later. Although she thought this bad timing, at least they were to be married shortly, and had their flat. She was however, afraid of telling her mum and knew it would really upset her but did not realise how much. Martha was all for cancelling the planned big wedding and the wearing of a white dress, until James, who normally kept quietly in the background, calmed the situation and persuaded Martha that the wedding plans should go ahead as no-one would know until after they were married. Sarah kept being terribly sick up until the wedding day and was anxious about how she would feel on the big day. However, by that time, the nausea had settled down and she did manage to keep her secret from everyone.

CHAPTER ELEVEN

It was her wedding day at last after a year of planning. The day was unusually hot and sunny for the time of year and Sarah, now feeling some relief from the morning sickness, was looking forward to getting ready. The bottom half of her dress was an A-line design in satin with a lace and satin bodice and flamenco style lace and satin sleeves. Her cap of Diamante studded flowers, cradled her mid-length red hair, which curled up and rested on her shoulders, and a long veil, scattered with lightly embroidered wedding bells, flowed from the back of the cap. When she was dressed in her full bridal outfit, James stopped and looked in wonderment at his daughter's beauty, which took his breath away. Smiling, he took her arm, and in his calming way softly asked, "Are you ready now?" It was one of the few times, she felt close to her dad. *'She is my little princess, at least for today,'* he thought to himself.

The young couple thoroughly enjoyed their day, as did all the guests. Everything had gone according to plan, now Sarah and Fraser were Mr and Mrs Todd. "Well darling," Fraser said, putting his arms around his wife's waist, at the end of their special day, "was it all you had hoped for?" Bringing out the actress in her, Sarah replied seductively, "It was great having top billing with you." Fraser laughed and drew her closer into a passionate kiss.

The next day, Sarah hung her wedding dress neatly in the wardrobe, and she packed her headdress and veil in a special box, carefully wrapping them in white tissue paper. She then placed the box under their bed for safekeeping. They had hired a car and honeymooned for a week at a castle-style hotel in the village of Invergarry, Scotland. The room had a large fireplace and king-sized bed. There was a small staircase in the centre with granite steps leading down to a sunken bath, big enough for two. Situated at the back of the hotel was a lake. At one side of the lake stood a rowing boat for the guests to use. Sarah thought it all very romantic. Being the grouse season at that time, the hotel, was inhabited, by, some extremely wealthy guests. She found them to be very friendly, not at all snobbish, as she had expected. They spoke perfect English and their clothes were well cut and classic in style. The food served at evening meals was new to Sarah and Fraser. They had never tasted grouse, venison or quail before and enjoyed sampling the new flavours. Sarah said she had felt like a celebrity. Their second week, they spent, touring, further up north to Skye and returning via Inverness. They counted themselves very lucky to have had the sun shining on them for the whole two weeks, being as this was quite unusual for Scotland at that time of year.

On their return home, Sarah and Fraser looked well, healthy, and very much in love. However, their bubble of happiness was about to burst. When they arrived at their flat, in the early afternoon, they noticed the lock was broken and the door standing slightly ajar. Entering with much trepidation, what greeted them was quite a shock.

Most of their wedding gifts (some still unwrapped) had gone. Their beautiful front bay window had been smashed, and the wardrobe doors were hanging off their hinges. While Fraser 'phoned the police and a glazier to board up the window, Sarah frantically flitted around checking what was missing. Her wedding dress had gone and she quickly crouched down to check under their bed. She pulled out the box with her veil and headdress and felt relief that at least they were still there and intact. The floor was covered, with paper, broken glass, and ripped clothes. There was also wet patches on the floor and the couple dreaded to think what this might be. Worst of all, Sarah's jewellery was missing, including two precious antique rings left to her by one of her beloved aunts. She ran into Fraser's arms and sobbed. He held her tightly for a few minutes until she composed herself then 'phoned James to come and take her to his house for the night, while he dealt with the police.

It was late when Fraser arrived at James and Martha's house. He slipped into the spare bed beside Sarah feeling very tired, as it had been a long day. She was still awake and he encircled her in his arms where she again wept. "Well, at least we are insured," he said, trying to brighten the mood. "Try not to worry Cuddles, we will get through this."

The next day Martha, James and William went over to help clear up the mess and at least make it a wee bit more habitable. Then, over the next few months Sarah and Fraser bought more items for the house, together with cot, pram and baby clothes ready for the arrival of their baby and settled into married life. However, the feeling of their home having been *'violated,'* still lingered.

Married life did not run smoothly for the couple. When Sarah was very heavily pregnant, she'd had enough. Fraser refused to help with the shopping or hanging out clothes to dry. "This is woman's work," he said in a dictatorial manner. Her hormones raging, she stormed out of the marital home to go back to her parents. Martha and James were both very upset and tried to persuade her to, at least talk it over with Fraser. Then, seeing how upset and exhausted she was, they decided to stop pressurising her, allowing her to stay with them in order to have a good night's sleep. During the night, a distraught Fraser came knocking at their door, asking if they had seen Sarah. They let him know she was, in fact, with them and safe. Advising, that all the upset was not good for her, and that they would get back to him in the morning after she'd had a good night's rest, and calmed down. He was not at all pleased with this situation, and angrily returned home.

The next day Sarah was still of the same mind-set, and, as far as she was concerned, James was driving her back to pick up her clothes from the marital home never to return. She started packing, as her father stood downcast in the doorway of the lounge. She saw Fraser sitting hunched in an armchair, tears silently running down his face. Her heart softened and the anger was gone. She walked over and encircled him as close to her as she could, given the size of her bump, and they were reconciled. James nodded and smiled at his daughter then turned to walk out quietly closing the door of the flat behind him. Breathing a sigh of relief, he returned to tell Martha the good news.

On the 23rd of March, three days before Sarah's 21st birthday, baby Daniel was born. He had large pale blue eyes and like his mummy, a head of thick red hair. When James saw his grandson, he could see his own mother in him and it was definitely her eyes looking up at him. He felt both sadness and joy as he pictured her face and thought about the little time she'd had with her own granddaughter, before her passing. Daniel was the pride and joy of both parents and grandparents alike. He was such a good baby and, given his colouring, everyone thought he was as pretty as a picture. Three years later, he was followed, by brother Craig, who was not at all like Daniel. He was a long thin baby with arms and legs that seemed to go on forever, and a head of brown hair. Martha said jokingly, "He looks like a greyhound." Unfortunately, poor Craig suffered rather badly with eczema and cried constantly, thus, wearing his parents out.

Fraser and Sarah had been very happy for a time after the birth of Daniel. Two months before Craig was born, they had moved, with the company Fraser worked for, to Huntly, a small town in Aberdeenshire. The first thing Fraser did was install an alarm system throughout. There was a lovely large garden, filled with all manner of flowers, shrubs and bushes. At the back of the house was a large expanse of lawn, fantastic for the boys to play on and the adults to relax sunning themselves on glorious summer days. Sarah looked after the garden and learned the art of caring for the different types of flowers and shrubs. She found she enjoyed working the earth and got great satisfaction in seeing her flowers and plants grow and thrive. The house had three bedrooms so plenty of room for their growing family.

Huntly was very different to Aberdeen and Sarah enjoyed all the social aspect with friends and neighbours. She had taken up flower arranging classes, and, entered a few of the shows in and around Huntly. Also, jam making (having picked the berries with Fraser and the boys), and sewing, were a source of enjoyment to her. She won many prizes for all three, acquiring first prize categories in the flower arrangement sections, which especially pleased her.

On the 29th of July 1981, Prince Charles and Lady Diana Spencer were to marry. Many organisations were decorating their offices in celebration of the wedding. Sarah asked Fraser if she might decorate his office window, and decided to use her headdress and veil. These were still, securely packed in the box since her own wedding. She unwrapped the tissue paper and looked lovingly at the sparkling cap, remembering her own special day and glad to have the chance to show it off once more. Carefully, the headdress was placed, over to one side, of the office window, then, the veil laid out artistically, along the ledge, in order to show off its beauty. In the centre, she placed an array of colourful flowers, which she had skilfully arranged in a container. A few keepsake ornaments, purchased to mark the special event, stood here and there on the veil. Sarah stepped back to admire her window arrangement, feeling very pleased with the end result. Many people stopped to admire the window display and commented how beautiful it looked. At this time in her life, she felt extremely happy and fulfilled. However, it was not long before she found herself pregnant again and feeling that it was difficult enough to look after the family she had, was not at all happy about the situation.

After the birth, Sarah became very ill. She so wanted a baby girl and was disappointed when Anthony was born. She took no interest in the baby and felt continually nauseous along with intermittent bouts of diarrhoea. Suffering also with depressive moods, and tiredness, she quickly became extremely thin. Luckily, Anthony was the type of baby who slept most of the time and Fraser fed, changed and nursed him each morning then put him back in his cot to sleep. He came home each lunchtime and repeated the regime, also looking after him and the other two boys each evening. After four months of this, he was so worried about Sarah that he 'phoned the doctor asking him to pay a visit. The kindly doctor sat on the edge of the bed, and sympathetically explained to Sarah that she was suffering from post-natal depression. After his talk with her, he prescribed a course of tablets to help with her recovery. He also said he would check on her from time to time to see how she was progressing. Now, with a bit more understanding of her symptoms, she immediately felt a lot better. It took some time but gradually over the next year, she felt more like her old self and was able to look after her family once more.

Fraser kept a tight rein on the finances, which Sarah had always been pleased to allow him to do, this being his job within the insurance company. He was now manager of the Huntly branch, which not only involved him visiting farms and businesses, all around the area, but also dealing in finance. The allowance he had always given Sarah for the children was not now enough, and, she struggled to buy them the food she thought they should have, and any new clothes they needed. However, Fraser would not give her another penny. She accepted his judgement on this, as he was the one who paid the bills, so trusted he should know how much could be set aside for the family's needs. She did wish however, that he would be a little more flexible at times with the money he allowed her to have. She found Christmas particularly hard, trying to give decent gifts to her three boys. They did always seem to be happy with what they found in their stockings from Santa Claus, and for this, she was thankful. There was one wonderful time she remembered, when she had bought raffle tickets for a charity and won the first prize of £200, she was able to buy a brand new bicycle for each of the two older boys, which was a real luxury for them

"She told me she fondly remembered that Christmas as being one of her happier times with the family. While talking to me, her expression changed, as she recalled a strange time with Fraser. A time in fact that was to be her downfall."

On that particular day, she had an appointment at the doctor with Anthony so Fraser had agreed to pick up the two older boys from school. It was a sunny day so he decided to walk. After collecting the boys, he was making his way home when he met an old work colleague from Aberdeen. "These are my sons," he said. The friend answered, "They don't look anything like you so, must look like their mother." Fraser had always been a jealous man and was already suspicious of his wife's infidelity (this being all in his imagination). The comment planted further to the seed of doubt already in his mind. During the next few days, he scrutinised his sons and thought his friend was right, he could not see anything of himself in the two older boys. Daniel was just like his mum, and he loved him for that, but Craig did not look or have any mannerisms of either his wife or himself, or so he thought. Little Anthony was the spitting image of himself, so there was no doubt there. The uncertainty about Craig began to gnaw at him. He had long since developed a jealousy of any man approaching his wife, but now began to think she might have been pregnant with another man's baby. Was Craig really his son?

It was around this time when Fraser had started to go out most nights drinking with his business friends. This seeming to be the normal in the small community, making Sarah feel that she was bringing up their children on her own. She loved the boys but dreamt of a much-needed night out with some adult company, thus the arguments began again between them.

On one of these boozy nights out, Fraser had come home the worse for drink and Sarah was annoyed with him. She started niggling and things got out of hand. An argument ensued when Fraser felt that she goaded him just a little too much. He lost his temper and without thinking, raised his hand, landing a hard smack across her face but immediately regretting it. He walked out to calm down feeling extremely guilty and vowing never to do that again, no matter how much he was provoked. However, the damage had now been done, and was causing the rot to set in within their marriage. Anthony, who had been sitting at the top of the stairs, heard the arguing. He stayed quietly in this position until his father had left then came down to his mother. He put his arm around her and said, "Never mind mummy, I love you." This comforted her a little as she held her hand up to her sore, bleeding nose. The next day she looked in the mirror and saw that her nose had swollen and her eyes were black and blue. It was at that moment, when she first realised she was now afraid of her husband and what he might do to her in the future.

CHAPTER TWELVE

William did manage to get into the Scott Sutherland School of Architecture, and had indeed, become an architect. This meant, however, moving away from the family home to Elgin for work. Martha had, to finally, let go of her baby boy. She was very proud of her son, but it felt odd not to have him around.

William was still very close to his sister and drove the twenty-six miles from Elgin to Huntly once a fortnight to have a meal with Sarah and some play time with his nephews. They had great fun with William and thought him the coolest uncle in the world. Sarah looked forward to these visits and the welcome time spent with her brother, especially as she saw less and less of her husband.

After one of these visits, on a frosty December evening, William was driving home when his car hit black ice and started to slide to one side. He quickly turned the wheel in order to try to straighten the car but overcompensated. The car skidded, turned on its side, and was then thrown against a line of trees, by the side of the road. Pictures of his loving mother, father, sister and nephews flashed through his head then there was nothing.

The news devastated James and Martha but Sarah felt she had to be strong for them all. She went to Aberdeen for a week to comfort her parents, and help with the funeral arrangements. It was a bad time for all so Sarah took herself off to the park to sit quietly with her own thoughts. While there, she suddenly spotted a familiar figure in the distance. As it grew nearer she realised it was Darren. At his side were two little girls. They were obviously his daughters as they too had his fair hair and looked so like him. As they came closer, she noticed the girls also had green eyes just like their daddy. It cheered her up to see him looking so happy even though a pang of jealousy shot through her, as she would have loved a daughter, and he had two. It never entered her mind that perhaps he would have liked a son. They happily talked for a while, (being interrupted now and then with the lively chatter of the little girls), before going their separate ways once more. After, on leaving to go back to her parents, she felt lighter of heart for seeing Darren, and meeting his two lovely girls.

Since the birth of Anthony, Sarah had suffered some depression and had not felt herself for some time. Things had become worse since the death of her brother, and were getting her down. With virtually no help from her husband, she was finding it hard to cope. One night, she just snapped. After yet another argument with Fraser, she threw some clothes into a very large carrier bag, not being in possession of a suitcase. Then proceeded to take some money, meant for new clothes for the children, from an envelope and, for one night only, booked into a bed and breakfast, situated on the outskirts of the town. At first, Fraser merely watched then shouted sarcastically, as she walked out, "How could you just leave your sons!" This was another of his remarks to make her feel bad and she slammed the door shut before striding off angrily.

While at the B & B she had time to think about what to do next. As the night wore on and she began to think rationally once more, she realised she could not leave her children no matter what the cost to her own wellbeing. She had spent a sleepless night and by the time dawn broke had made her decision. She paid the bill and walked slowly home. She plucked up the courage to confront Fraser saying, "I am only back until the boys are old enough to look after themselves as I have fallen out of love with you." Fraser, realising he might be losing Sarah, desperately worked hard over the next few weeks to get back into her good books.

By coincidence, an insurance policy, which Fraser had taken out some years earlier, had just matured, and he thought this good timing. He decided to use the money to arrange a family holiday to Paphos. It was booked for April and was to be their first holiday abroad.

As the time grew near, they were all excited about flying for the first time. A self-catering villa had been booked near Coral Bay and it was only a short walk to the beach. They all enjoyed the holiday very much and everything was a first-time experience. They loved the brilliant blue colour of the sea, the golden sandy beach, and the little tavernas where they ate mezes. However, most of all they revelled in the hot, sunny weather. So, happiness had returned once again, for a time, to the Todd family.

CHAPTER THIRTEEN

It was Sarah's practice to drive to Aberdeen once a month and spend the day seeing her parents. As there were only a few shops in Huntly, she would also take the opportunity to go to the city centre, for some clothes shopping. On one of these occasions, while in town, she spotted Rosie. Sarah thought how slim and happy she looked. When Rosie turned and saw Sarah she smiled, throwing her arms up, and waggling them in the air with a little scream of joy, then they both ran and hugged, squeezing each other tightly. They went for a coffee, and talked over old times catching up with one another's news. It was wonderful to see Rosie again, and she listened intently, surprised to find out that Rob and Rosie had split up for a year. However, Rob had finally confronted his stepmother and told her that he wanted to be with his wife and daughter. He had given her the ultimatum of either accepting this or losing him forever. The couple had reunited and now had another son as well as twin baby boys. Sarah sat spellbound, so this was why Rosie looked so well, she was very pleased with this news and happy for both Rosie and Rob. The two friends decided they would now keep in touch, thus, their two families met up now and then in Aberdeen spending time together, usually going to the swimming pool at Hazlehead Park. In this way, the children of both families also became friends and they too, looked forward to their get-togethers. Sarah very much enjoyed these outings. Fraser was hesitant at first, which annoyed her, but he relented and the Black family's fun, being infectious, spread to Fraser and her boys, or at least on the days they all spent together.

Back at home, from time to time, on their own, Sarah again started to notice a change in Fraser's mood when he would suddenly, for no apparent reason, become very sullen and quiet. If she spoke to him during these low moods he would shout at her, making her feel inadequate. As she had a busy life with the children, she tried to dismiss this strange behaviour telling herself he was just working too hard.

In truth, Fraser had started to think that his middle son did not look like him at all nor could he see any traits of himself in him. The seeds of doubt were growing and he began to wonder if Sarah had had an affair, and it was eating away at him. He felt that Craig was a very untidy boy and lacked discipline. When he tried to chastise his son Sarah would step in and always go, against what he tried to do, or at least this is how he saw it. The feelings of rage grew towards Craig and Sarah felt that Fraser's treatment towards him, compared to the other two boys, was unjustified

Unfortunately, Craig was a trying child. He had tantrums, told lies, was often untidy in his dress, and at home, but no matter what, Sarah loved him. He had shiny, brownish, straight hair with a fringe, which had a mind of its own, always seeming to hang down over his eyes even after several attempts by Sarah to brush it back. When he grinned from ear to ear, Sarah knew he was about to get up to some mischief. An example of his boyishness was, when Sarah was washing the dishes in the sink, above a cupboard where the cleaning materials were stored. Craig had spilt something on the floor and was trying to wipe it up but not very successfully. "Come on," she called, "give it some elbow grease." Sarah then carried on her conversation, which she was having, with Daniel. Suddenly she was aware of Craig pushing her out of the way to get into the cupboard.   "What are you doing?" she asked, in a frustrated voice, puffing out her cheeks. "Looking for the elbow grease," he said in a serious voice. Sarah and Daniel looked at one another and burst out laughing, but Craig could not fathom out what was so funny. This was part of Craig's charm and she loved him even more for his naivety. His grandma Martha called him her *'Angel with Tackety Boots.'* He was good for nothing, but seemed to have a natural talent for doing and saying silly things that made them all laugh, all that is, except Fraser. His dislike for poor Craig was growing more with each passing day.

CHAPTER FOURTEEN

In her twenty-eighth year, Sarah had been stricken with influenza. It had laid her low for a month with continual coughing, which had caused her muscles to go into spasm, making her fingers and toes curl up tight. The GP had given her an emergency injection of cortisone to relax the muscles, and finally she began to get better. For a few years after this, on and off, she would suffer flu-like symptoms with sore limbs and feel extremely tired. It was rather frustrating, while trying to live a normal life, as both a housewife and mother, to young lively children, but she struggled on. Each time she attempted to explain her symptoms to a GP, Sarah received no answers. She began to think that all the doctors believed she was imagining them. Sometimes she found it extremely hard trying to deal with the normal family routine, and her tiredness and pain, while also trying to calm the situations, which arose between Fraser and the two older boys, especially Craig. It was taking its toll on her, 'I find it hard to remember any of the good times we had as a family now,' she thought to herself, sighing.

Fraser played golf most weekends, therefore, Sarah and the boys would be left, to fend for themselves. This caused many arguments between them, but Fraser refused point-blank to change his routine. Sarah often thought of the one rare occasion, many moons ago, when they all went a drive in the car and stopped for a walk in a wooded area they had come across on their travels. The two boys ran on ahead to explore, then came back, circling their parents and baby Anthony, being pushed in the buggy. They suddenly emerged into a clearing where the sun shone on the most beautiful carpet of wild flowers covered in fluttering butterflies. She remembered how Fraser's face lit up and he whispered, "It's out of this world. I've never seen so many butterflies in one place." They spent a couple of happy hours in that heavenly, unusual part of natural land but, for some unexplained reason, were never able to find it again. When she was feeling low she would close her eyes, transport herself back in her mind to the magic of that day and for a short time, things would seem brighter.

When Craig was eight years old, he had taken up playing the recorder. The headmistress at his school had suggested that Sarah and Fraser should both encourage his eagerness to play, as he seemed to be a natural. He was showing an artistic flair recently as, not only did he enjoy playing the recorder, but had started to draw many wonderful sketches. Sarah thought, at long last he was now doing something of which she and her husband could be proud.

On one particular afternoon, Craig had just finished classes for the day, and told his friend he would not see him until early evening as he had a recorder lesson. On his way he realised he had left the recorder at home. Being as the family home was not far from the school building, he checked his watch and decided he would have time to fetch the musical instrument before his lesson.

The chimney had been cleaned the previous day, and Fraser had also nipped home between visits to farming clients. This was in order to lift and dispose of the large black pieces of plastic sheeting which had been laid, to protect the carpet in the lounge. However, he had at that moment, received a 'phone call from Craig's teacher saying that he had forged his parents' signature on his homework, yet again, and asked Fraser to please speak to Craig about this. Fraser became incensed.

At that moment, Craig appeared. He walked over the shiny sheeting towards a small table which stood beside a rather imposing black granite fire surround. There he picked up his recorder. "You're at it again." Fraser boomed in Craig's face, "being underhanded and forging your mother's and my signature on your homework so that we won't see how badly you're doing." As he shouted, he pushed at Craig's shoulder knocking him backwards. Taken aback by his father's outburst, Craig slipped on the plastic flooring. Falling backwards, he cracked his head on the hard granite fire surround where he lay still. "Get up," boomed Fraser again. Blood trickled from under Craig's head. Fraser knelt down and shook him then felt for a pulse but found none. The blood stained his hands. "Oh my god, I've killed him," he yelled panicking. Although it had been an accident, he knew Sarah would not believe him because of the ongoing arguments he'd had lately with Craig. She would never forgive him and he just could not bear to lose her. He needed Sarah, his hunger for her was like a drug of sorts, far stronger than anything he had ever encountered in his life. He paced the floor, and wringing his hands, while sobbing the uninhibited tears of a child, knew he had to get rid of the body, but how?

He tried to calm down and think rationally. Finally, a plan began to form in his mind. He looked up at the clock on the wall. It was 4.30 pm. Sarah was visiting a friend with Anthony and he knew she would not be home until 7.00 pm and, being Friday, Daniel was allowed to stay overnight with a friend. If he was quick, he could do it. He wrapped the piece of plastic sheeting, on which Craig lay, around the small body and carried it out to the boot of his car. The car had been parked in the garage, which had an adjoining door to the house, so he knew there was no chance of neighbours seeing, but thought most of them would still be at work anyway. He then went back into the house, collected the rest of the plastic sheeting and popped this into the bin. He picked up Craig's recorder, putting it into his pocket. He also collected a garden spade and his DIY dungarees to protect his suit, then put everything into the car. He thoroughly cleaned the blood from the fire surround, with a mixture of oxygen bleach and liquid flash, in the hope that no bloodstains, through luminol application, would be detected at a later stage. This was something he had learned through his interest of crime scene investigative reports. He then placed the bloodstained cloths into a plastic bag to be taken to the car and disposed of. When he was happy that no sign remained of what had occurred, he locked the front door and drove off.

He drove as far away, as time would allow, to a thick wooded area where he put on his dungarees and special elasticated covers over his shoes, making a mental note to dispose of these also, and acquire a new pair. Then, with the spade, shaped out some clods of grass covering and dug a reasonably deep hole. He then rolled Craig's body from the plastic sheeting into the freshly dug earth, shovelled the earth back into the hole and carefully placed the pieces of saved grassy covering back, in order to look as natural and untouched as possible. He thought of some areas, which he had come across while going from farm to farm in his business capacity. These, he knew, would be ideal to hide the sheeting and cloths. He remembered one such place being part of a very old farm out-building, which had been left to decay and fall into disrepair until only one wall was left, with part of an old drain pipe buried under stones and moss. Drove on then stopped the car and again put on the shoe coverings. These he used tramping around the farms when working. He walked over to the pipe into which he stuffed the piece of plastic sheeting, which had encased Craig's body, together with the bag of cloths. Completing the task, he covered the entrance with more stones and moss. Finally, he travelled a little further on and flung the recorder into the centre of a small pond, another discovery he'd found on his travels. Happy that he had done all he could to cover his tracks, he drove home as quickly as possible, cleaned the spade and put it back into the garage. Finally, he checked his appearance, then, calmly drove on to meet with his last farming client for that day. He convinced himself he had done the right thing in the circumstances, and tried, as best he could, to totally dismiss from his mind, the part he had played in his son's death, albeit accidental, and the cover up thereafter.

When Sarah arrived home, she was pleased to see that Fraser had binned the plastic sheeting and tidied up the lounge. She started humming to herself happily while she got little Anthony ready for bed. She loved to cuddle and play with him in his pyjamas after his bath, just before she finally laid him in what he called his *'big boy bed.'* She tucked him in with his special cuddly toy (a brown knitted dog with a tiny scarf wrapped around his neck and a sewn on smile), while thinking how small he looked in his new bed. 'He was growing too fast,' she thought sadly, and would all-too-soon, grow, to better fit it.

When she came into the lounge again and looked at the time, she wondered why Craig had not arrived home yet. It was now 9 pm, which was late for him. She decided to 'phone his best friend, Graeme. "Is Craig still with you?" she asked, "and if so, tell him to come home now as it is getting late." "He said he'd come round in the early evening after his recorder lesson but never appeared." Graeme answered. "Okay then," was her reply and now feeling a bit anxious, replaced the receiver. She was really starting to worry now. When Fraser arrived home, she ran frantically to him saying that Craig was not home and he had not gone to Graeme's house, as had been his plan. "Right then, you 'phone round some more of his friends and I will go back out and drive around to look for him. Perhaps he is hanging about outside with some of his other friends," Fraser replied. He drove off round the corner where he sat parked in his car for a while, before going home, pretending to have looked for his son, but having found no sign of him. Sarah, by then, was even more frantic, and had now come to the conclusion that it was time to 'phone the police.

By this time, the news of Craig's disappearance had reached the ears of friends and family, who had in turn, related this to neighbours. By 11 pm many of the people in Huntly were out looking for clues as to his whereabouts, lighting up the darkness with their torches. Searching throughout the next day also, some even drove to the outskirts of the town in their cars in order to widen the search. Fraser became a bit apprehensive but he had buried the body quite deep and covered his tracks well. Sarah, thinking how helpful everyone had been, was overcome with emotion, while at the same time, being filled with renewed hope. Sadly however, her hopes were dashed, when no trace of Craig was found.

The police took a full statement concerning the missing boy, as far as they could, together with an up-to-date photo. For the next few weeks, the police force searched, questioned and interviewed but came up with no leads. The last time anyone had seen Craig was after his final lesson at school. It then seemed as if he had just disappeared into thin air. There had been no reports from any of the neighbours having seen him arriving at his house. Sarah, was totally, distraught, and so was Fraser, or so she thought. He certainly was giving a good impression of being so. Their little boy was gone, had he been abducted or worse, would they ever see him again?

Over the next few months, Sarah went through all sorts of emotions from sad to angry and guilt to depression. Little Anthony, who was picking up, on the family's grief, became ill. He was continually vomiting, and as was keeping none of his food down, became extremely thin. The family doctor realising this, decided to have him taken into hospital whereupon he was drip fed for a time. Daniel was also feeling the strain, and it was showing in his schoolwork. Finally, Sarah seemed to come out of the deep dark place she had been living in since Craig's disappearance, as she realised she needed to 'get a grip of herself,' for her family's sake if nothing else.

Now it so happened, at this time, Fraser had been offered a promotion. This being in the form of a new position in Glasgow. Although Sarah still lived with the hope that one day Craig would return, she agreed with her husband that it would be better to have a fresh start for them and their two boys in a new town and so, the couple took the decision to move. Before leaving Huntly, Sarah ensured that the detective in charge of the search for Craig, had their new address, and made him promise to get in touch if there was any news of her precious son.

CHAPTER FIFTEEN

Prior to their move to Glasgow, Daniel and Anthony enjoyed visiting their granddad Whyte and they were very interested in the war stories that James told them. They related some of the stories to Sarah and she now began to understand, a bit more, her father's feelings for the need to have peace and quietness. While she was growing up, he had felt the memories of the war still too raw, so had never spoken of this to her. She laughed when the boys explained, that her dad had started as a corporal in the Home Guard, making her think of the television comedy, 'Dads Army' and picturing her father getting up to the same antics shown in that sit-com.

James, as a very young soldier, was firstly, trained in Aldershot, on the Bofor guns. These were the large guns used to protect the towns against mortar fire. After six weeks of training, he was posted to Dover early in 1942. Dover was known as, 'Hell Fire Corner,' because of all the action taking place there. When he arrived in Dover, every rail station had an RTU (return to unit), giving directions to all the soldiers. James reported to the RTU saying he had to join the 129th Royal Artillery Regiment. He was then told, that the headquarters of this regiment, was in a building, only a few yards along the road. When he arrived, they were expecting him, but as it was 2 am, he was advised to spend the night there, and in the morning, he would join number four gun detachment situated on the white cliffs of Dover.

During the night, the *'Cuckoo'* warning was sounded, thus alerting that the German big guns were firing from beside Calais. One shell landed in number four pit and killed all four men there. If James had been there one day earlier, as he was scheduled to be, he too would have been killed. After this episode, he had a few other near death experiences. Although never actually having been wounded in action, he was, badly injured in a nasty accident when one of the Bofor guns broke free of its housing. It rolled down catching James unaware, crushing one side of his body. As he was young, strong and healthy, he made a good recovery after being out of action for some time. However, this was to have an effect on him in later life. That day, one of his kidneys had in fact, been destroyed, and the other was only partly functioning, but he had no knowledge of this at the time.

Also in 1942 James was posted to Southwold where there were quadruple guns (four guns stretching out high in each direction) and he operated the Bofor gun, positioned 50 yards from the quadruple guns. This was to help stop the deadly mortar before reaching the land and the men manning the quadruple guns. At that time there was persistent mortar fire from the Messerschsmitt (ME 109's as they were called) which was German fighter aircrafts. As James fired the Bofor gun, he felt his helmet slip down over his eyes with the constant vibration, and prayed he was still shooting at the correct target. This too, must have been a frightening experience for him.

When he was in Berlin at the end of the war, where there were displaced units of soldiers from different countries, he, and some fellow soldiers from his regiment, had gone to see Hitler's bunker. This was being guarded by one of the Russian soldiers at the time.

The big burly man waved his hands signalling *'no,'* and, as he was a strong looking brute, they did not pursue it. As they turned to go James had mumbled, "Sod you," at the man. He suddenly felt the Russian's hand on his shoulder and thought he was in for a beating. Thankfully, the truth was that the Russian had noticed a pack of cigarettes in the pocket of James's uniform and, was only after them in exchange for allowing James, and his comrades to enter the bunker. Thinking back, he was glad that he'd had the chance to see it before it was completely obliterated from the site. The German Government did not wish there to be any future constant reminder of Hitler having been there.

The boys were told many other stories by James, some heroic, some funny, some macabre and some very sad, but all were extremely interesting and they were very proud of their granddad. Sarah's heart softened towards James when she realised that her dad, had actually, been awarded several medals, but that he had, in fact, refused them. It had been his belief, that every man and woman, engaged in the war, be they off fighting for their country, or, helping out, at the home front, were all heroes in their own right and deserved medals. He held a strong feeling that it was unfair for these medals to, be given only, to members of the Forces, therefore, he refused to claim them.

CHAPTER SIXTEEN

Early, on the morning of the Todd family's departure to Glasgow, Sarah quietly opened the back door and stepped out. She stood on the lawn and looked at their house, thinking of the good times as a family before Craig's disappearance. She recalled the sunny days on the lawn with the paddling pool, and visualised Craig and Daniel splashing in the water happy and laughing. Craig with his cheeky face and grinning from ear to ear, about to push his brother back into the water. She could also remember them both running and jumping on the lawn with their football, pushing each other over to get possession of the ball and rolling about on the grass howling with laughter. The memories of this caused her to collapse to her knees, the tears again welling up in her eyes and running gently down her cheeks. "Oh Craig, my darling boy, where are you," she whispered. She said a silent prayer for him and hoped wherever he was he was safe. Fraser watched her from his position inside the house within the shadows at the side of the lounge window. He loved her so much and hated to see her so sad, but, adopted the attitude what was done was done, and could therefore, not be undone.

At that moment Sarah remembered a quote she had once heard, *'We must be willing to get rid of the life we have planned so as to have the life that is waiting for us.'*

She then stood up, composed herself, and taking a tissue from her jeans pocket, wiped the tears from her face. She turned around to re-enter the house, then taking her husband's hand, she called for Daniel and Anthony that it was time to go, and they all walked out of the front door for the last time.

Fraser had already spent six months in his new job in Glasgow prior to the family moving there. He had found the perfect house in a good neighbourhood on the south side of Glasgow, in readiness for the family's move. All that remained was the transportation of their furniture to their new home.

The day after they had moved was Daniel's birthday, and, being near the end of March, he managed to attend the new primary school for eleven weeks, before the summer holidays. This worked out well as it enabled him to make new friends before starting secondary school in August. Sarah had not been sure how he would settle but she needn't have worried as he made lots of friends, and really enjoyed his new home. He still missed his brother terribly, but did not talk of it. He was trying to be brave for his mother's sake. He had taken to speaking to Craig in the privacy of his own bedroom, relating the news of the day, as a way of keeping his brother with him always.

They all settled into their new life. Fraser had already been in Glasgow finding his way around and learning his new job so, he was well clued-up. However, wee Anthony, not yet being of school age, was rather bored. He had been used to a full programme of pre-school activities every day in Huntly, and was not attending anything in Glasgow. He was an inquisitive child and liked to be on the go, trying out new experiences daily. Sarah found him quite exhausting at times, but did finally manage to get him into a playgroup a couple of days a week, for six months prior to starting school. There, he settled down, becoming more content and back to the happy little boy he used to be.

For the next few years, Sarah enjoyed several group activities and made new friends, enjoying the freedom of being a stay-at-home mum while her boys were at school. There was plenty to see and do in Glasgow and the shopping was fabulous. Shows were a new thing for her and she particularly loved the pantomimes where performers like Rikki Fulton, Gregor Fischer, Stanley Baxter, Tony Roper and many others starred, all of whom she had only seen on TV. It was so exciting, to actually see them live on stage. She found the Glaswegian people to be very friendly with a good sense of humour. She was also amazed at how the people of Glasgow, even though some were poor and had very little to be thankful for, were always ready to help others and still managed to laugh at life.

"Oh," Sarah exclaimed.
"At this point remembering another part of her life."
"I remember also our pet."
"She proceeded to tell me about the time they decided to get Daniel a pet. A smile lit up her face and I could see how happy this pet had made her."

It was not long after they had moved to Glasgow Sarah noticed how down Daniel was about his brother and mentioned this to Fraser. "Why don't we get him a pet to look after," he said. "Well, if we mentioned that, he, like most children, will want a puppy and I think that would be too much for me," she answered. When they spoke to Daniel, they made sure he understood that it was to be a small pet and that he would be responsible for it. The decision was then made to get a long-haired golden hamster. Fraser's dad, a carpenter and pattern maker by trade, kindly designed and made a large two-floor cage for the hamster. Three sides were made of wood and there was a front Perspex panel. Small steps led up to the top floor and there were special clasps to attach the water bottle and food container. It was a beautifully crafted piece of work, and certainly seemed, to be very much enjoyed, by the small furry animal. Daniel named him '*Little Craig*,' after his brother.

Little Craig lived a few years, but after a time Daniel grew more and more disinterested so Sarah took over. She cleaned the cage once a week and made a run on the lounge floor out of old film recorder video cassettes, standing them upright. She also dotted, here and there, cardboard from the centre of toilet rolls, for him to run through. She fell in love with the lovely soft furry creature and his antics. There were a few times, when he escaped out over the video cassette walls, going missing for one or two days at a time. The family would search and search but to no avail. Then suddenly they would hear him gnawing at something. One time, he was found, to have escaped through a crack in the floorboards. Another time he had gnawed a hole in the fabric underneath the sofa leaving a rather large tear in the fabric.

"At this point, I noticed how Sarah pursed her lips and sucked in her breath as she remembered how furious Fraser had been at the time."

In April 1982, Fraser had gone on a golfing holiday with friends, leaving Sarah on her own for a week. The two boys were at school on this particular day and the hamster had gone missing again. Sarah had searched and searched, but was unable to find him. She had some shopping to do so decided to resume her search for the little creature, after her shopping trip.

On her return home later, with her arms full, she had left the front door slightly ajar. A flash of fur shot past her feet as Little Craig raced out. She turned to shout to him as he ran into the road. He stopped and stood up on his back paws to sniff at the air as if realising he was free. Suddenly a speeding car came round the corner crushing the hamster under its wheels and sped on. Sarah, on witnessing all this, was horrified. She dropped the carrier bags of messages, and looking around, quickly picked up a small lidded box, which Anthony had left lying at the foot of the stairs, then ran out. The sight of the small area of crushed bones, blood and fur would haunt her throughout her lifetime. 'This was all my fault,' she thought to herself, feeling full of guilt and sadness.

"Some people may think of this as only the unfortunate accident of an animal and nothing else. However, to Sarah he was more than a pet, he was part of the family, and, a friend who had given her so much fun, soothing that part of her which ached for her missing son."

Slowly, she bent down and scraped up what she could of the remains into the box, covering it with the lid. She did not have the heart to tell Daniel what had really happened so firmly taped the lid shut, keeping the box so that he could bury his pet in the garden when returning home from school. When the news was broken to Daniel that the hamster had simply died, he too, felt quite sad but accepted it more than his mother had.

"At this point in our session, Sarah paused and looked down at the floor from her seated position. She was quiet for a while and her face again filled with despair. My heart went out to her."

CHAPTER SEVENTEEN

Sarah started back to full time secretarial work when Anthony was eight years old and was, by then, glad to do so. When she returned to work again, her first company owners, who were not of a Christian faith, were very strict, and although she enjoyed the company of her colleagues, she did not care much for the way the staff were treated. She then went to work at an engineering company and found the treatment of their staff very different. She thoroughly enjoyed her work and remained there for several years. She was secretary to one of the Directors who, although worked her hard, was fair. He also had a sense of humour, '*as she related in a story to me*,' of the letter which had a typing error, '*bugger.*' Her boss had written in the margin '*bigger,*' whereupon she had retyped the correction as '*BUGGER,*' but thankfully, he simply laughed it off. However, after a couple of years, a new man took over as Chairman of the company and changes, were made, but not for the better. There was a huge turnover in staff as they became disillusioned with their new job positions, including Sarah.

She next started working for a financial adviser. It was a new company with one other male employee, George, and another female, Eva, who had been brought in, to, job-share with Sarah. The boss (Mr Crichton), was very nice to the ladies, but completely changed his manner when talking to George. Sarah felt sorry for her male colleague. Other things, in the day-to-day running of the business, were not, carried out in a very professional manner, and Mr Crichton was a rather fat, balding, lazy man, a bit Dickensian. Pay cheques for both George and Eva bounced a number of times. Mr Crichton was always shouting at George about his work, and, although no sign of his work being poor, was ever shown, he was sacked. Later that same month, Eva flounced in one afternoon, when Sarah was working, and told her she was handing in her notice. Her pay was not in the bank, yet again, and because of this, she felt that she'd had enough.

Sarah was now, left on her own, in the office, with this strange man, who was her boss and, she was rather apprehensive about the situation. Her desk, was positioned, as a unit in a corner of the room, with only one opening from which to get in and out. Mr Crichton would stand over her each morning, rather too closely, and while he opened the mail, she would feel his breath on her neck. He would also hover in this position as he read the financial times, staying put so that if Sarah wished to leave her desk for photo-copying etc he would deliberately, it seemed to her, only move a few inches meaning she had to brush up against him in order to pass. It sickened her to her stomach. Several mornings, after removing her coat in the cloakroom and brushing her hair in the mirror, she was aware of him standing watching her and it felt decidedly creepy. On one of these occasions, he came over and made a big show of brushing away a loose hair from her shoulders. She felt extremely uncomfortable with this, and even knowing that she had no real reason for thinking he was sexually harassing her, did not feel right about it all. After a month of being on her own with him in the office, feeling rather frightened for what he might do in the future if she stayed, she too decided to leave. After handing in her notice, he thumped his hand on her desk, making her jump, and asked why she was leaving. A shiver ran through her, and she lied (which she never did), saying that there was just not enough work to keep her busy. It was her wish now, to look for a position, which would use her time more effectively. This thankfully, he accepted, allowing her to leave with a good reference. She breathed a sigh of relief, when her final day came to an end, and she was able to leave the building, and that terrible man, behind for good.

"This all happened during a time when staff did not report sexual harassment in the work place. If you wished to keep your job, you had to simply put up and shut up."

In 2002 Sarah started working in what was to be her final position, before retiring in 2010. This was in the secretarial department of a large infirmary situated near her home proving to be very handy for travel purposes. She loved the buzz of the hospital and got on very well with her colleagues. Here, in the secretarial department, her job was to 'pick up the slack,' when there were too many letters for the consultants' secretaries to type, on top of their other duties. Sometimes, when the consultants' secretaries were off ill, or on holiday, temporary staff were taken on, and they would find some of the words difficult to decipher on the tapes. Sarah and her colleagues would have to check these letters and burst into fits of laughter when they read some of the misinterpreted words or sentences such as:-

a) Discharge status: Alive, but without my permission.

b) Patient's medical history has been remarkably insignificant with only a 40 pound weight gain in the last three days.

c) Patient had waffles for breakfast and anorexia for lunch.

d) She stated that she had been constipated for most of her life until she got a divorce.

e) Examination of genitalia reveals that he is circus-sized.

f) The lab test indicated abnormal lover function.

g) She has no shaking chills, but her husband states she was hot in bed last night.

h) Between you and me we ought to get this lady pregnant.

There were lots more of these hilarious mistaken medical words and phrases found in the letters, which kept Sarah and her nursing colleagues in stitches (pardon the pun).

CHAPTER EIGHTEEN

Daniel, had been a slightly chubby boy, and because of this and having red hair, he had not had much in the way of confidence in himself, especially when it came to communicating with girls. As he reached his mid teenage years, he lost this puppy fat and developed a trim physique and square jaw. He had become a very handsome young man. He loved singing, and as three of his friends were musical, playing lead and base guitar, and the drums. They got together and formed a group with the name, *'Crushed Monkey.'* Sarah had a chuckle at that, and wondered how they decided on that name. Daniel would bring home recordings of his friends playing their instruments, and, while listening to it - **at a rather high volume**, would add his own lyrics. Sarah found the music loud and not to her taste until one day, she heard a recording of the group singing, *'Sweet Child of Mine.'* She asked Daniel what song this was and he replied, "It's by the group Guns and Roses." Sarah liked it very much and thought the guitar solo at the start was fantastic. From that day, this song was to become her favourite and each time she heard it she would break into a frenzied type of dance. She had not appreciated how good her son and his friends were until then. They began to play gigs and Daniel grew his hair longer, down to his shoulders. Sarah thought how beautiful his hair actually was, so thick and shiny with a natural wave through it. Many girls would give their right arms to have hair like Daniels. His confidence grew, and the girls loved him, going wild when he shook his head of hair vigorously at them, while singing on stage.

When Daniel was in his seventeenth year, he started college to study for a degree in Hotel Management. Sarah and Fraser had tried to dissuade him from this, thinking he could do something better with his qualifications, but his mind was made up. After completing his degree, he started work as a deputy housekeeping manager at a large hotel in Glasgow and moved out of the family home, into a flat, which he shared with three others. He had always been a very capable, tidy boy, and fitted into the sharing routine very well, enjoying the new learning curve of freedom and looking after himself.

After two years in the flat, he decided to have his long hair, cut short. He applied for a new post as head housekeeper, in a hotel in Jersey. After interview, he was delighted when he received a letter of acceptance in the post. It was at this time the Crushed Monkey group had decided to break up, as the friends were all moving to different parts of the world with their respective job prospects and ambitions. It had been a good couple of years but it was now time for all of them to move on. They vowed to remain friends, hoping to meet up again, at some point in the future. It was the end of an era and the beginning of adult lives for the four young men.

Daniel had settled into his job, and, recruited some new maids, to work in the hotel during the summer season. These girls were all from various universities, working to accrue some money during their summer break. Daniel especially liked one girl, who attended Kent University. Her father was from Goa and her mother from Kent. Her skin was light brown in colour, she had long shining black hair (which she tied back in a ponytail when working), beautiful white teeth when she smiled and the loveliest, velvety, deep dark brown eyes. Her name was Corina, and Daniel had taken quite a shine to her. When talking to the invisible Craig one night, he told him how much he liked Corina and that he had asked her out twice but she had said, 'No,' "Probably because I am a redhead," he chuckled. "But this will not deter me, and I'll keep trying 'til I wear her down." Corina at last relented and actually enjoyed their first date, finding Daniel made her laugh. She was surprised to find just how much she wanted to go out with him again. "I finally won her over Craig," he announced happily to his brother that night in the privacy of his own room.

CHAPTER NINETEEN

Anthony had grown into a lovely little chap with a happy-go-lucky nature. He was an intelligent boy who did well academically at primary school and had many friends. The girls especially, loved him, as they considered him very handsome, with black hair, bright sparkly dark blue eyes and long eyelashes.

"Sarah had a thing for long eyelashes and wondered why boys seemed to be born with this more so than girls."

They also found he had a good listening ability, hearing all their woes, and dishing out good advice. His mum thought he would have made a good counsellor.

When he was twelve years old and had started secondary school, his persona changed. He met in with a girl named Angel (but no angel by nature). His parents on meeting her one night took an instant dislike to the girl and were not keen on him continuing the relationship. However, Anthony dug his heels in and kept up their friendship. She led him a merry dance while getting him into so much trouble. He mixed in with some of her friends who were of a dubious nature, and started smoking and drinking. However, he was clever enough to avoid being caught by either Sarah or Fraser, who thought their son was whiter than white. Daniel lovingly called him, 'The Golden Child.'

One of Angel's ex boyfriends, who still thought of her as his, grabbed hold of Anthony one evening and knocked him to the ground face down. Anthony was not a fighter so thought he was clearly for it. After being punched several times, his face hitting the ground, the result was a broken and bloodied nose. When he came home, he had cleaned what he could of the blood onto his handkerchief and tried to creep up, without being seen, to his room. His parents however, were standing at the top of the stairs. They were shocked to see their son's face and suspected a broken nose. They took him to accident and emergency, where, this was confirmed. He told them all about Angel and her friends' exploits and they forbade him to see her or her so-called friends again, by which time he had actually decided this for himself.

After this episode in his life, Anthony was restless and wanted very much to leave home and live on his own. At the age of fifteen, he decided to take up a place at a university in Aberdeen to study for a degree in computer science. He had all the qualifications needed for this and saw no reason to do an extra year at secondary school. It seemed very sudden to Sarah and she knew she would miss her youngest son very much. When he had gone, she still looked for him coming home from school in the late afternoons and felt the house empty without him although, she had been at loggerheads with him for some time before his departure. She thought about how much he had changed in the last year and hoped that going out on his own in the world would perhaps calm him down a bit. He had been very eager to leave the nest and perhaps this was what he needed. She hoped so as the doubts came into her mind, thinking of her missing son. However, this was not to be the case.

For the first year (Freshers) Anthony enjoyed his freedom. He shared student accommodation with two messy girls (unusually, for a man, **cleaning up after them**), was partying, drinking, and even got a tattoo of a small scorpion on his back, but he drew the line at taking any kind of drugs. He was also missing lectures and falling behind in his studies.

At the start of his second year, he took stock of his life and decided it was time to change. He knuckled down to study for the next two years and completed his degree. His parents, of course, proudly attended the graduation ceremony and had no knowledge of his initial year of self-destruction. They were quite surprised to find out about this in later years, when hearing it discussed with his brother while attending a family party.

At the Todd's house, Fraser had started noticing black spots in the vision of one of his eyes, which worried him. He made an appointment to see his GP who in turn sent him to see a specialist. After some tests, he was diagnosed as having toxoplasmosis. This had apparently developed while a baby in his mother's womb when, she had been cleaning out the litter trays belonging to her father-in-law's cats, and served as a stark warning to other women to be careful of this when pregnant.

Over the next few years, the sight in Fraser's eye became worse and he had developed blind spots. He was still able to drive but did have the constant worry of losing the sight in his other eye in the future. After a few years, the decision was made, by the consultant in the eye clinic, to try a trio of drugs. It was hoped that this may help his condition, and hopefully, stop, any more scarring within his eye. On his admission to hospital, he was started on the trial for a couple of days, then, allowed home to continue the treatment for a further two weeks, before being re-assessed. However, during that time he developed some strange physical manifestations. He felt flu-like symptoms, which worsened over the next few days. At the end of that week, his mouth and face had become swollen, he was not able to eat or drink and he felt extremely unwell. He happened to say to Sarah that he'd found it strange, when being discharged from hospital, that they had only given him two of the drugs to take, but as he had no medical knowledge at that time, he trusted they knew what they were doing. She then took him back to hospital where, he was immediately, secluded, into a special oxygen tent. It was discovered that the oversight, was destroying the white blood cells in his body, which fight infection, therefore no visitors were allowed, not even his wife or children, for fear of further infection. Fraser was seriously ill and the consultant in the ward said he could have died had he waited any longer to return to hospital. It took quite a while for his white cell blood count to return to normal, but he did manage to survive which was a relief to the family.

During this very worrying time for Sarah, her mum and dad came to stay in order to help out, by taking care of the children. The hospital was a three-quarter hour drive away from her house and it was during the month of January, when darkness descended early. On the first of her nightly visits driving to see her husband, her dad sat beside her for the journey, this being the first time driving on a motorway since she had passed her test. It started to snow heavily and laid a covering over the road signs. Sarah had made a wrong turning off the motorway and felt lost. She could not read any of the signs covered in snow and started to panic. James, in his usual caring way, tried to calm her down. "It's alright," he said soothingly, "keep calm and drive on a bit until we can get back onto the motorway. You can do it." This was one of the times she was glad to have her dad at her side.

After this episode, Sarah too, was having health problems. The pain in her limbs seemed to be lasting for longer periods of time, and she had also developed a shakiness in her neck. To her relief, she was finally given a diagnosis of fibromyalgia, and torticollis. She went through months of various treatments, injections and medication, finally settling on a routine with pain-killing medication from her GP, and exercises given by the physiotherapist. She was informed, that there was no miracle cure, and that things would probably get worse in the future. This news left her feeling extremely downcast. However, being the optimistic character she was, eventually she accepted her fate and learned to live with it as best she could. Her motto being, 'There were always people worse off than you.'

Fraser lived for his golf and played every weekend up until his retirement whereupon he tried to play four days a week. In between, he did some gardening and other jobs around the outside of the house, keeping himself busy. He, was lucky enough, to have been given the chance, of an early retirement package, at the age of fifty, when his company was merging with another organisation. This was too good a chance to pass up, so he decided to accept it. Sarah worked on part-time at the hospital until she was sixty then she too retired. She still managed, up to a fashion, to do her keep fit, so was reasonably happy to see her friends at classes and have more time to do her housework. She continued to think about her missing son, and, also longed for grandchildren, secretly dreaming of a little girl. However, deciding that it would be lovely just to have any, no matter the sex, before the symptoms of her dreaded fibromyalgia potentially became worse, which would inevitably hamper any physical play with the little darlings.

CHAPTER TWENTY

Corina and Daniel had now moved from Jersey to jobs in London, renting a house in Richmond and were living quite happily together. Corina's mother and father had long since divorced, as it had not been a happy marriage, given their different cultures, and the split up was quite acrimonious. Corina's mother, Jennifer, had moved back to Kent and her father, Vishal, had stayed in London. He originally came from Goa at the age of seventeen to attend university, where he met Jennifer and ultimately became an accountant. Jennifer, Sarah and Fraser all travelled to Richmond, for a few days, in order to see Corina and Daniel and become acquainted.

Sarah and Fraser initially found Corina to be complicated, a multi-faceted person. She was a very pretty girl who came from a moneyed family, seeming a bit domineering and used to getting her own way. She came over, as quite serious and quiet but would then become louder as she talked and laughed. Her accent was very English, and the Todds, being Scottish, found it difficult to be on, the same wavelength, when trying to have a joke with her. She also had trouble understanding some of the Scottish accented words. Sarah and Fraser kept an open mind and tried not to form too much of an opinion as their son seemed so happy in the relationship. Jennifer on the other hand, was found to be a soft-spoken lady, with a lovely nature, and they very much liked her from the start.

That Christmas, when all the family were together and had finished the traditional Christmas meal, Daniel decided to have a bit of fun with Corina. He had bought a quiz book where the questions were in Doric (very broad Aberdonian language) and handed it to Corina first to peruse. Everyone was in on the prank and waited to see her reaction. While looking over the book she ran a hand distractedly through her glossy black hair, with a quizzical expression on her face. After a few minutes of trying to understand the questions, she decided, and announced, quite seriously, "I think, with a little help, I would be better to act as the quiz master," and they all dissolved into laughter.

Daniel was not happy working in London. He longed to get back to Scotland but did not wish to upset Corina by saying this. However, he managed to persuade her to move to a flat in York and Daniel was happier there for a while. Finally, Corina agreed to move to Glasgow where they rented a flat for a year until they decided whether they would stay. Corina had graduated, as a teacher in London, but owing to a different system in Scotland, was not happy teaching in the school in Glasgow. The children came from poor backgrounds, the school building seemed to be falling apart, and the headmistress was rather old fashioned in her teaching methods. She therefore decided to leave teaching and got a job working in the Human Resources department of Strathclyde University. There, she did well and was promoted quite soon after. During this time, Sarah and Fraser familiarized themselves more with Corina. Although she liked to take control in the household affairs, which Daniel was happy to allow, she was a hard worker and loved him very much. Daniel too, was besotted with Corina, "We make a good team," he beamed at his parents. They whole-heartedly agreed.

Daniel and Corina both loved Glasgow and settled there, buying their own little flat. While on a short winter break in Prague, Daniel proposed to Corina on Christmas day and she said, "Yes." Sarah and Fraser were very happy at the news but there was no plans made in the short term for the wedding as the young couple wished to save up first. They lived happily and always seemed to get on very well doing everything together and having the same interests. They were not only lovers, but also very good friends. They seemed to have the perfect partnership, unlike Sarah and Fraser.

While at university, Anthony worked at a bar situated on the promenade at Aberdeen beach to earn some money. He practised throwing the bottles up in the air on the sand, in case of breakages, and when he had mastered this he enjoyed showing off his skills behind the bar. Situated in the building next to where he worked, was a restaurant where a bubbly blonde girl was manageress. Anthony got chatting to her one day, asking her name and introducing himself. Then Tiffany, as she was called, started to come into the bar, in order to see him for some chat, at the end of her shifts. Although there was a few years difference in ages this did not deter them getting together. Dean, who also worked in the restaurant and through Tiffany, became great friends with Anthony. The two young men both had the same interests in common and participated in many sporting activities together. Anthony was happy with Tiffany, and his friendship with Dean. After about a year however, Anthony thought Tiffany was getting too serious and pushing him towards marriage. He felt he was too young for this and, to Tiffany's dismay, finished the relationship. She became quite unhappy and each night after work idly slouched around her flat, vowing to wait for him.

There were many girls after this for Anthony, he was very popular, and for a while enjoyed their attention. However, in time he realised he missed Tiffany and that she, was the one for him. He contacted her and they met for a long chat. This culminated in the renewal of their relationship, whereupon they moved in together, he at least making some commitment, if not marriage, and this pleased her.

As part of the university course, the students had to work out for a year and Anthony excelled in this. By the time he had finished his degree, he had attended five interviews, and was offered all of them. This was partly because the companies liked the idea that he had work experience. Thus enabling him to be lucky enough to have the choice of what he thought to be the best employer for advancement in his career, and so, settled into this position. When he had gained enough experience, he left to start up in his own business. This he did with gusto and built up his clientele through his good work and trustworthiness. Tiffany helped in his company by doing the accounts and keeping the books, part time, in between her own job. By which time she was now driving around parts of Scotland managing the franchise, which had grown from the original restaurant.

Things were going well for him and he booked a week's holiday in Prague for two, where he also proposed to Tiffany (just as his brother had done previously to Corina). They then planned the wedding for the following year in early September.

Both the wedding ceremony and reception were to be at Maryculter House hotel, where the ceremony was to take place out in the open. The grounds were beautiful with clusters of trees just starting to show the autumn colours. Flowers still displayed some of the last of their summer blooms, and a small river gurgled past in the background. The couple were not sure if the weather would be kind to them. However, they need not have worried as, although the morning was cloudy and dull at first, the rays of sun split through the clouds shrouding them in sunlight, while saying their vows. It was a magical moment and this, they hoped, was to be a good omen for their marriage. They were very photographic, as a couple, and with such a scenic backdrop, the wedding photographs were quite stunning.

CHAPTER TWENTY-ONE

Two years later little David was born to Anthony and Tiffany. Sarah was over the moon she finally had a grandchild. Since the announcement of the pregnancy, she had spent many happy hours searching the shops for baby clothes and filling a special, 'New Baby' presentation box to give to the couple after the birth. He added a new joy to both Fraser and Sarah's lives. They did not see him as often as they would have liked, as he resided in Aberdeen and they in Glasgow. However, they looked forward to the times when they were together, revelling in the excitement of finding each time that he had grown that little bit more to reach a new stage in his development.

Daniel and Corina had now arranged to be married at a church in Ayr (Burns country), having the reception at the Brig O Doon House hotel. They had a great interest in Rabbie Burns and his life and work, and had therefore, planned their wedding day around this theme. The tables were set with the names of his poetic subjects, and a small book of his poems was handed out to each of the guests. The couple were also thrilled to have some of the wedding photographs taken on the fifteenth century Auld Brig O'Doon. This being the setting for the famous poem, in which Tam o' Shanter was chased by the witches, and where he had headed on his horse Meg, who, it was told, lost her tail while fleeing with her master across this bridge. It was versed, that Tam o'

Shanter knew that the fiendish creatures could not cross running water.

The whole day had gone perfectly, and Sarah had never seen Corina looking so beautiful and feminine, in her shoulderless dress, her hair swept up at the back of her head to where a small veil was attached. She was usually such a tomboy. Even the minister said he had to look twice to recognise her. There was also a surprise for Sarah at the reception. She was overcome with emotion, when Daniel and his friends took to the stage where they proceeded to sing and play, 'Sweet Child of Mine,' dedicating it to her. The friends had enjoyed playing together one more time and the guests thought they were brilliant. The four young men were ecstatic when they finished their performance to rapturous applause by the guests who were all upstanding.

David was now eighteen months old and had the biggest, bluest eyes and blonde hair. He looked so cute dressed in a kilt for the occasion and was full of smiles throughout. His grandparents watched him proudly. He had such a lovely nature but his parents still had trouble getting him to sleep at night.

Unbeknown to the rest of the family, a rift was starting to form in the relationship between Anthony and Tiffany and their lack of sleep, caused by David, did not help matters. Tiffany had become pregnant again and went on to have a second son, Michael, which compounded the problem. Dean, having married also, had moved down south and no longer kept the same contact with Anthony, who missed chatting to his friend. Sarah loved visiting her two grandsons but started to notice the change in her son. He had become serious and distant. She could see there was no love or happiness between her son and his wife anymore and was extremely worried about them both, not to mention the affect it might be having on her grandsons.

Anthony had started to come every couple of months, on his own, for the odd weekend to Glasgow. While there, he would meet up with Georgia, an old friend from school. Although Georgia had been married, and Anthony and Tiffany had become friends with the couple, she had now separated from her husband. Anthony and Georgia were very close but only as friends. One evening, when they were meeting for a meal, she had invited her new boyfriend and a single girlfriend to join them. The evening had gone well and they had all enjoyed themselves, having had quite a bit to drink. Georgia's girlfriend, Sheila, shared a taxi home with Anthony as their respective destinations were close to one another. Sheila invited Anthony in for a coffee and became very flirtatious towards him. Anthony then pulled her closer and they kissed rather too passionately. Suddenly Anthony realised what he was doing and stopped himself. He, was not that kind of man and would never betray his wife in that way. He gently pushed Sheila away "I'm sorry, it's not that I find you unattractive and perhaps under different circumstances......" he said hesitating, "But, I am married with two lovely boys and cannot do this." Sheila reluctantly understood and Anthony thought it best to leave.

Some months later, Anthony and Tiffany decided to start afresh, by emigrating to Australia. Although Sarah was happy for them, as they were trying to work things out and save their marriage, she was also very sad to be losing her grandchildren. When the time came, they all said their goodbyes at the airport, with much hugs and tears, promising to SKYPE. The young family gave a last wave and disappeared to board the plane. Sarah took Fraser's arm and in silence, both deep in their own thoughts, walked slowly back to where they had parked their car. Not a word, was spoken, between them, as they travelled home with heavy hearts.

Sarah and her husband very much looked forward to the SKYPE sessions. These sessions were few, and far between. The two young boys would become restless after five or ten minutes, pressing buttons on their daddy's equipment. Anthony had set up an office in a room in their new house, and did not usually allow the boys in except to SKYPE, with his strict supervision. Their young curious minds however, would cause them to touch what they should not. Sarah found she was becoming more and more anxious for the boys with each SKYPE so suggested, with a feeling of sadness, that it might be better for all concerned if they stopped contacting in this way.

Now, Sarah was feeling her aches and pains more than ever and an overwhelming feeling of gloom. As the next few weeks passed, she felt very depressed, then, something happened to cheer her up. They had received a wedding invitation, to Rosie's oldest son's wedding. As the bride to be, lived in Huntly, that was where the wedding was to take place. Sarah was delighted to be meeting up with their old friends again and although was slightly saddened by thoughts of her lost son, was excited at the prospect of seeing their old home again. Fraser, on the other hand, was very apprehensive. He did not wish to resurrect memories of that part of his life which had been buried deep in his subconscious mind.

On the day before the wedding, at Sarah's request, both she and Fraser arrived in Huntly. They took a walk round to see their old house then went for a drive around the outskirts of Huntly. This was near to where, some years before, Fraser had buried his middle son and dismissed it all from his mind. He was pleased to see that the land was unchanged, looking exactly the same. Then, as if a tap had been turned on in Fraser's head, the events of that fateful day, came flooding back.

Sarah very much enjoyed the wedding, and seeing Rosie and all her family again. She returned to Glasgow in a much better frame of mind, but not so Fraser. The trip had affected him badly.

CHAPTER TWENTY-TWO

Over the next couple of years, Sarah noticed a change in Fraser's behaviour towards her. He became irritable when she asked questions or put forward opinions on things, standing unnecessarily close to her and shouting in her face, his eyes dark with rage. He would also complain about her cooking, the sauces were either too watery or too dry, rice or pasta had no sauce at all, and there was not enough taste, or seasoning. Another source of her berating was for wasting hot water, and spending too much money on what she thought was only necessities for the household. There was not the same intimacy or closeness from him anymore and she thought he had fallen out of love with her. Her confidence plummeted and she shied away from meeting friends, consequently, becoming a recluse in her own home. She felt sequestered in a marriage that was now a sham and sequestered in a body and mind that were no longer working, feeling foreign to her.

During his berating moods, her heart would suddenly beat faster and she started to get panic attacks, which left her fighting for breath. The worst part was, that on the few times they had sex it was always on his terms. There was no softness or love and, in her words, 'she felt like a whore.' Now and then however, Fraser would, revert back, to his old self, becoming tender and loving with gentle caresses, which, although pleasing, only served to confuse Sarah even more.

"I suspected at this juncture, that these few times, were when he, in his troubled mind, felt remorse and was trying to atone for what he had done."

She hated to admit it but she now feared her husband. Her yearning, to, again be loved, was overwhelming. Now she had reached a point where there was no happiness for her, it was a living hell.

Sarah loved her sons dearly and above all, she wanted them to be happy. Therefore, she did not divulge to them, any of her physical pain nor her mental state relating to the unhappy marriage.

"However, considering how she had looked when first I set eyes upon her, I could not believe that Daniel did not suspect something to be wrong. Anthony on the other hand, now living abroad and not seeing much, if anything, of his mother, might not have been aware of her situation.

One of the happier times Sarah recalled to me, was Hogmanay 1999 on the eve of the Millennium."

Both herself, and Fraser had arranged to have the night out with Rosie and Rob. They spent the evening at a nightclub on the beach promenade. The club had three floors of entertainment, one of which presented an Elvis Presley tribute act. Rosie adored Elvis and was enraptured by the performance, the joy lighting up across her face. Later, they went on to walk up Aberdeen's main street in the city centre. Union Street was lined with a plethora of different stalls and musical entertainment for the special event, and everyone thoroughly enjoyed themselves. At the stroke of midnight Fraser, having a cold sore on his lip at the time, decided to be sensible and gave first Sarah then Rosie a hug. Rob on the other hand, kissed Rosie then slowly and deliberately put his arms tightly around Sarah giving her a long lingering kiss. In all the years she had known him, he had never kissed her before, not even a small peck on the cheek and although taken by surprise, did feel flattered. This had aroused

Fraser's jealousy and because of it, Sarah suffered his dark mood for a few days thereafter.

"She did say to me however, that it had been worth it and how she remembered the night with fond memories. Little did she know the misery Fraser was feeling. The guilt for Craig's death was mounting up inside him and he hated himself. He was not sleeping well and the pictures of his son and what had happened played over and over in his mind, making him feel as if he was going insane. He could not see how his wife could love him, and was distancing himself further and further from her because of the wretchedness he felt. Every day he wanted to unburden himself to her but couldn't, it was all-consuming like some parasite slowly eating away at his body bit by bit."

In the midst of all the unhappiness however, a wee light shone. Corina and Daniel, having been on holiday, had come to visit Sarah and Fraser on the pretext of showing some holiday snaps. These so-called photos turned out to be a baby scan picture, and the realisation that Corina was pregnant, dawned on them both. They were to be grandparents again, and Sarah prayed that this might help to lift Fraser's continual dark mood. Corina and Daniel had now moved to a house in the same area as the potential grandparents, so hopefully, they would surely see more of this grandchild.

Unfortunately, two months later, Sarah and Fraser's relationship had gone from bad to worse. She had tried very hard to please him but it was like shifting deckchairs on the Titanic. Nothing was working, so, she simply tried to accept the situation, and took things day-by-day. It was like walking on glass trying to keep out of his way as much as possible so as not to annoy him. What she had not realised was that In the meantime, he had descended into a very dark place.

Sarah felt great empathy for Princess Diana at this time, as she was also desperately unhappy in her marriage and as with the

Princess, she too had become bulimic. She would go on walks and purchase caramels, tablet, crisps and bars of chocolate and devour them with such greed, she gave herself no time to enjoy the sweet or savoury taste of the items. She would then go home and make herself sick to get rid of the offending sense of nausea. After this purging, she would feel so much better until the circle of loathing and destruction started again. At first, it was once a week, then it escalated to once a day and sometimes even twice. This self-loathing behaviour continued for about two years until Sarah came to realise, it was sapping all her energy and only adding to her feelings of worthlessness, she really would have to try to stop. Thankfully, she finally achieved this, although, as with alcoholics and drink, she continued to struggle with the temptation of food, which was always there.

Adding further to her problems, her dad had collapsed, and been taken to hospital. James was nearing his eighty-eighth birthday and feeling very much his age. He had been feeling tired of late and breathless with the slightest of exertion. What he did not realise was that his heart was giving out and his one working kidney was starting to fail. The hospital consultant decided to give him some tests prior to a new heart valve operation, which they thought might need to be carried out, and he was ordered to rest. It was during these tests, that the discovery of the problem with his kidneys, was finally found.

One day, while watching from his bed, during the stay in the new hospital unit, he was perplexed as to why the nursing staff seemed to look a bit awkward when turning on the long-handled taps of the sink in the ward. Through his plumber's eyes, he realised the taps had actually been attached the wrong way around. When Martha visited, he asked her to bring in some of his tools and proceeded to fix the taps. This was just like him, still helping others even to the detriment of his own health. Unfortunately, the exertion was too much, and near collapse, he was helped back into his bed. That evening, as Martha sat holding his hand on one side, Sarah kissed his forehead and lay her head at his shoulder on the other. Although it was a struggle, James slipped his free arm around his daughter and finally felt close to her. He was now content and smiled lovingly at the two women in his life then gave a last gasp, and passed away. After a few moments of silence, Mother and daughter held each other tight and quietly wept. The next two weeks Sarah felt completely out of her depth. She was overwhelmed with what had to be arranged after her father's death. Recognising her responsibilities, and for her mother's sake, she undertook, what seemed at the time, an enormous task to be done to close this painful chapter in their lives.

It was a blessing for both Martha and Sarah when Anthony and Tiffany returned to Aberdeen where they stayed for a month after the service, which was held at the Aberdeen crematorium. Her two grandsons had grown and developed so much and it was wonderful to see them both again. Tiffany was now in the early stages of her third pregnancy and Sarah could see how happy the couple now seemed to be.

"Sarah told me, she could not have had any better news at that time and I was inclined to agree."

Martha had ordered a long double-sided arrangement of red carnations and roses with a sprinkling of white flowers and green foliage, which was, draped along the top of the coffin. Sarah had chosen an arrangement showing, **'D A D',** in blue and white flowers edged with blue ribbon. Although the arrangements were beautiful and admired by the two women, it could not take away the deep loss they felt in their hearts, this being obvious for all to see.

On the day of the service, when the family car pulled up alongside the crematorium building. Sarah, was taken aback, when she saw a large number of elderly people making their way slowly towards the main door. She was filled with strong emotions when she realised that they comprised of: old friends of James's, '*Jimmy Boy*' as he was known then, formed during the war years; buddies from James's bowling days; and some old workmates. All had come to say farewell to their friend even though, they themselves, could not walk without the assistance of walking sticks and frames, paining them to do so. She swallowed hard as a lump came into her throat, not realising until then, that her dad had been, so well loved.

A eulogy was read by Anthony at the service, this being a surprise to both his mother and grandmother.

He walked up to the podium where he rested his notes then began. "I would like, if I may, to tell you about a man. A man who has been hugely inspirational to me throughout my life, but especially so during my adulthood. This is a man, who led many different lives, as a plumber, a soldier, a gaffer, a father and grandfather. He excelled in each, and every one of them.

He fought bravely during the second world war, and I assume, witnessed many of his friends and comrades die, I say, I assume, because he never actually told me so. He related many stories of his time during the war but they were always positive, designed to instil a feeling of warmth and optimism. This was typical of him. In all my years of knowing him, I never once heard him recount an unhappy tale or moan and complain (well, with the occasional exception of Aberdeen Football Club of whom he was an avid supporter)!

How many of us could honestly say that we would endure the horror of war and not feel somewhat bitter about the injustice of it all? Not him! He, saw the positives, he, was the lucky one. Not only because he survived the war, but, because he had also made good friends in the process. Some of those friends were lost during the conflict, but he simply saw it as a privilege to have known them at all. I can't help but wonder at how a man can be so consistently positive about life.

Not only was he positive but extremely modest with it all. He told stories from his life that simply astounded me but he told them as if they were nothing really, just an interesting or funny story. There aren't many people that can claim to have bribed their way past a Russian soldier with cigarettes into Hitler's bunker in the days immediately after the war as he did! I was in my thirties before I found that one out.

It was during these same first days following the end of the war that he assisted in transporting German soldiers as prisoners of war. Many of the British and Russian soldiers were brutally abusive to their charges. Understandable, I suppose. One could be forgiven,, for holding a grudge against those that have caused you so much pain for so long. But not this man. He saw the German soldiers as people no different to himself, just young men caught up in a war and doing as they were ordered to do. Rather than beat these men down, he shared some music and his chocolate rations with them. Such compassion.

He was awarded medals for his bravery and service but did not claim them. His feeling was that everyone, even those at home, all played a part in the war effort and all deserved medals. As far as he was concerned, he was simply doing what he had to do as best he could.

This attitude followed him in everything he did. Many years later, he was the plumbing supervisor during a refurbishment of Balmoral Castle. In order to give the resident Queen Mother a choice of all the possible colours available for the bathroom suites, (bearing in mind that it was all coloured suites in those days) he carefully arranged for a large display of all the options to be shown in one of the ballrooms. All his men were lined up eagerly awaiting the Queen Mother's arrival, anticipating her perusing all the coloured suites, and betting as to which colour she would pick. On entering the hall, she simply looked at him, somewhat confused and said, "I want them all to be white," and walked back out. A woman ahead of her time.

There were many more stories such as these that I was fortunate enough to hear about, but no doubt, there were many, many more that I didn't. So modest was the man that he genuinely didn't seem to realise how extraordinary his life experiences had been. More's the pity, as I have no doubt that he could have written a fascinating book. In fact, he was encouraged to do so but to no avail. Modest to the last.

This man is now lost to me, and all those who knew him, but his influence will live on in me forever. If I can be only a fraction of the man he was, then I'll be doing very well indeed.

I take a great deal of comfort in knowing, as he repeatedly told me over many years, that he was content and, in his words ,'I've had a happy life.' In the end, all that mattered to him was having his loving wife next to him, and that's exactly how it was."

The eulogy was delivered with such professionalism. Nearing the end, he looked up and saw Sarah and Martha wipe away the tears and for a few seconds his resolve broke down. Martha felt so sorry for her grandson and called out softly, "Go on Anthony." He composed himself, stood up to his full height and placed his hands on the podium. Then with much love and pride in his voice, ended with the words, "And that man was James Whyte, my granddad. Thank you granddad, for the happy memories, for showing me the kind of person who makes the world a better place, and for all the differences you didn't realise you made."

In these few moments Sarah now understood, through the words of her son, who her father had really been, and, she finally realised how privileged she was to have been his daughter. 'If only I had shown him more love and affection while he was alive,' she thought sadly.

"At this point in her story, it now made sense to me why I had heard the regret in Sarah's voice when first she had spoken of her father."

When the service at the crematorium finished, Sarah was astonished but pleased to feel Fraser slipping his arm around her saying, "He is at peace now." In that rare tender moment, she felt a closeness to her husband, which had been missing for quite some time and it gave her the smallest glimmer of hope for their future. However, there was to be no more, as it was the last time Fraser could muster up any love from his wretched troubled soul.

In the ensuing weeks, Martha was beside herself with grief asking over and over again, "Did I do enough to look after him?" Then cursing him for leaving her. Sarah helped her mum move into sheltered housing, hoping she would have some good years with friends met at the complex. When visiting Aberdeen again after a couple of months, she saw the palpable difference in her mum. Martha was so thin, she seemed to have shrunk in size becoming round-shouldered, and her clothes were hanging on her. She was not eating and had no interest in her appearance. She seemed to have lost the will to live and just wanted to be with James. This was not the strong woman, Sarah knew as her mother and she felt completely helpless. It was not long after this that Martha passed away.

Sarah now had another funeral to organise. Although this time she was better equipped, she felt so alone and wished with all her heart that her brother was still alive, to help share her burden of grief.

There were times, following this, when little things would remind her of her parents and she would find herself yearning to see them again coming through the door with their bright smiling faces. "How many more of my family do I have to lose?" She cried despairingly.

CHAPTER TWENTY-THREE

It was a Friday night when the bleeding started and Corina tried to rest and take things easy over the weekend. By Sunday morning, Daniel who, had by this time, become extremely anxious, took her to the maternity unit. A scan was carried out which sadly showed that the baby had died, and as Corina was six months pregnant she had to endure the painful process of labour. The baby was a boy. After a post mortem had been carried out, nothing untoward was reported, only adding to their grief. Sarah put her arms around both Corina and Daniel and could feel the heaving of their shoulders against her as they both quietly wept for their lost little baby. In that moment, Sarah thought that whatever she was going through, in her marriage, was nothing to what these two young people were feeling at their loss. A small ceremony was carried out for the baby and he was buried in a special part of the Linn crematorium where many unborn, stillborn, and babies who had not survived long, were laid to rest. As Sarah looked around at all of the graves strewn with flowers, teddies, and toys, she felt an overwhelming sense of loss and compassion for all the families of these lost little ones, including her own.

Very much feeling the need to record something of her lost grandson, she decided to write a piece of poetry as a sort of memorial to him. It was her hope that by doing so he would always be remembered.

You only lived to six months in your mummy's womb
Long enough to photoscan and fall in love with you
You lay there in the photo and we thought you were okay
It was not to be and now you've gone away
Thoughts of growing into a little boy and
Of what you may have brought to us in joy
You were never held or given a name
But Little One we loved you all the same

She then attached the poem, with tape, into an album where she kept photographs of her other grandsons.

"When Sarah recalled this part of her story to me, I remembered someone telling me, 'Every ending is a beginning, we just don't know it at the time.' I thought how, in that moment, I'd really like to believe this would be so, for this family."

Three letters fell out of a pocket at the back of the album, which she had forgotten about. They were a bit brown and spotted with age. She had forgotten about these beautifully, well composed, letters from Fraser expressing his love for her.

After finding the letters, Sarah went into a deep depression and when she heard any of these two songs on the radio, 'Without love I have nothing at all,' by Tom Jones or 'Just one smile,' by Gene Pitney, she would cry. She found herself crying quite a lot during the next few months, desperately craving the love she once had with her husband, while trying to think of the people who were much worse off than herself, but now nothing seemed to lift her spirits.

"It was at this point that Sarah's GP decided she needed some help and referred her to me."

She started to wonder, 'What if?' 'What if my primary school teacher hadn't been off so much prior to the 11-plus exam – would I have gone to senior secondary school and if so would I have done better?

What if Lizzie hadn't moved into my street - would I have studied harder and had a better education?

What if I had married Darren - would I have had daughters instead of sons. Ah but would I have felt fulfilled in love if I had not married Fraser?

What if we hadn't moved to Glasgow – would I have had different daughters-in-law?'

A wee smile then spread across her face as she thought of her three sons and her precious two grandsons. She knew she would never have changed that.

"During a visit to her GP in early 2010, it was decided that Sarah should be referred to me for counselling. Slowly, over many months of talking, the dark cloud, which had been hanging over her for so long, started to lift. By February 2012, she was beginning to feel better about herself again and this is when I first saw her smile. Her once haggard face was now starting to become more youthful, and her eyes looked alive again. The short, cropped, hairstyle she now sported, revealing her petite ears, had a sprinkling of natural blonde spreading through her fringe, longer at one side, now and again catching her eyelashes. I remember thinking how attractive it looked, when the remaining red parts of her hair glinted in the sunlight streaming in through the window where she sat. I felt great satisfaction then, to have had a part in helping this human being to once again, enjoy life.

Parts of her story she had related to me however, were only what she herself imagined, for example, what visions had run through her brother's mind in the seconds before his car crashed, and what thoughts lay behind her dad's final smile."

CHAPTER TWENTY-FOUR

During the sessions with Amelia, Sarah had not mentioned much of Fraser's parents and she was curious to know why. When asked about them, she answered.

"Their names were Patsy and Mike and in the early days of meeting them I liked them very much. Patsy was a glamourous woman who always liked to look her best and Mike thought the world of her. As I got to know them better, I realised Patsy was a rather selfish woman who got all her own way and Mike indulged her, allowing it to happen. They liked to do everything together, having a good social life and always enjoying themselves. When Fraser was in his early teens, he was, quite often left alone in the house. What I found strange, was that although they were, wrapped up in each other, they tended to argue a lot. I felt sorry for Fraser, and when their grandchildren, our sons, came along, they had little or no time for them either. My annoyance then became great and I had as little as possible to do with them. However, I wouldn't have wished their lives to end the way they did."

"Sarah then paused and I gave her a quizzical look, whereupon she continued."

"They were holidaying in the States and visiting New York at the time of the World Trade Centre attack and were killed. I tend not to think or speak of them now."

"I gasped and expressed my sincere apologies for the pain I may have caused in asking about them, and stating how sorry I was for the way in which they had died. Sarah uncaringly shrugged her shoulders and left it at that."

CHAPTER TWENTY-FIVE

In the late autumn of 2013, when quite some time had passed since the sad demise of their baby, Corina was now six months pregnant again. She had been keeping in good health and all seemed well with the pregnancy. Both she and Daniel had decided to wait before announcing the news to everyone. That night they were intending to go over to tell Sarah and Fraser.

It was 11 am, Fraser had just finished his game of golf and was sitting in his car parked outside the golf club. The vision of his son lying with eyes bereft of life, and blood oozing from the wound on the back of his head was again in his mind's eye. His thoughts drifted back to a day in December when he and Sarah were driving out Lanark way to see some Christmas displays at the garden centres. He had decided to overtake a bus on the motorway when it started to veer out with no warning and tore off his inside wing mirror, but it could have been worse. "Sarah, or myself, or both of us, could have died in that incident and I need her forgiveness for what I did," he said out aloud to himself. He then came to the decision that he would go home and tell her the truth about everything connected with Craig's disappearance and the part he had played in it.

"It was at this time, on the last two sessions with me, Sarah had been thinking a lot more of Craig, and told of how she hoped he was happy wherever

he was. She refused to believe he was no longer living and kept the thought alive of seeing him again one day. I realised that this was important to her recovery and hoped very much that it would prove to be the case."

When Fraser arrived home, Sarah was in the kitchen chopping vegetables for lunch, and singing along to songs on the radio. She had been feeling a good bit better lately with the counselling sessions, more like her old self but, was completely unaware of what was about to hit her. He put a hand on each of her shoulders and turned her around to face him, whereupon he proceeded to blurt out the whole, sorry tale before dropping to his knees. With tears running down his cheeks, he looked up into her eyes and begged her forgiveness.

"Ironically, at the same time, the words of 'Forgive me please, I'm on my knees, I've been a bad bad boy,' as sung by Paul Jones of the Manfred Mann group, was being played on the radio in the background."

In that few seconds, he had taken from her, the hope she'd held for years, of seeing her son again. While processing this unbelievable turn of events, like the clashing of the earth's tectonic plates, a rumbling started in the bowels of her guts, then, a magma-type spewing of emotions rose up through her body, culminating in a tsunami of reactions awash in her brain, destroying any reasoning or rational thoughts. This man, whom she had loved unconditionally, trusted and cared for, had betrayed her. Not only had he psychologically, abused her for some time, but had also killed their son, and, for all these years, let her believe that Craig might still be alive. It was just too painful to comprehend. All her love for Fraser, together with any hope of ever seeing her lost son again, was now completely destroyed. She felt the knife in her hand and lifted it to plunge deep into his evil heart. Then she felt a searing pain and clutched her free hand to her chest. This final shock to her already frail body, weakened with years of pain and grief, had been the last nail in her coffin. Her breathing stopped, and the knife slipped to the floor.

"In the corner of the room appeared a strange light and from its midst two figures approached, one with its arms outstretched. Sarah recognised her granddad Fraser and beside him stood Craig. Once again, she felt the feeling of love and warmth, as her granddad enveloped her in his arms, while her long lost son, with his cheeky grin, looked on."

Fraser cradled the now lifeless body of his one true love in his arms, and started to cry, just low broken whimpers at first then sobbing as if his heart would break. How, could he live with this, he had now committed two murders, albeit accidentally. In his mind, he was responsible for the death of two human beings. Two members of his family, he, was meant to love and care for. He knew now it was all over. He laid his wife's arms gently at her side and whispered, "I love you so much and am so terribly sorry for all the pain I have caused. You are at peace now and once again happy in the bosom of your family." He gently kissed her on the lips for the last time and sighed deeply, before raising himself up. Assuming a stooping gait, he walked over to the table where a pad and pen lay and determinedly composed a very long letter to Daniel, explaining everything. He then 'phoned Daniel asking him if he could come over later that evening, to which Daniel replied, "Of course dad, I had intentions of coming anyway as I have some news for you and mum." On hearing the word 'mum' Fraser flinched as a chill ran through his heart.

After the call, he slowly walked to the door. He turned, and forlornly looked back at Sarah then, with the steps of a man much older than his years, quietly closed the door, leaving it unlocked for Daniel, knowing, that whatever happened next, it could not possibly be as bad as that which he had endured over the last few years. The torture he had caused himself over a throwaway comment from a work colleague, having planted a seed of doubt, and, in turn, had grown and torn his family apart. Now it was time to pay and finally close the thirty one year old missing child case. Getting into his car, he then sped away, disappearing into an early evening mist, which had descended around the area.

"This fact was reported later to Daniel, by a neighbour, who had been passing at the time."

That evening when Daniel arrived at his parents' house with Corina, they were excited about the news they were about to impart. Daniel thought it a bit strange when he noticed his father's car was not in the drive, considering their visit was expected.

They walked up to the door and rang the bell, but there was no answer. Daniel pressed down the handle and found the door unlocked so he walked in. "Mum, dad, where are you?" he called. Again, there was no answer. He went to the kitchen and was shocked when he saw his mother on the floor. He quickly bent down to feel for a pulse but her body was already growing cold and rigid. "Oh mum, what happened?" he cried out, as Corina looked on horrified. "Where is dad?" He shouted distraught, then turned his head to look around for answers. The pages, torn from the pad and strewn out on the table, written in his father's handwriting, caught his eye.

CHAPTER TWENTY-SIX

S ix months later Daniel made an appointment to meet Amelia.

"He came into my office pushing a buggy containing a sleeping infant and holding some folded papers in his hand. He introduced himself then told me some more of Sarah's story."

"My mum kept me informed of her counselling sessions with you, and how you helped her. For that I am grateful."

"He then handed me the papers he was holding."

"This is a letter which was written by my father just after Sarah died. I am sure she would have liked you to know how her story ends, so please read it."

"As I read through the sheaf of papers, I got more of a sense of why this man had ultimately treated his wife so badly, even though he appeared to truly love her. He wrote of his feelings from the time of meeting Sarah and before and after Craig's demise. He told also of looking into her eyes and how, he'd seen exactly what her emotions were and of seeing the knife stiffening in her hand, when he had begged her forgiveness. In that moment, he knew she meant to kill him. However, the most mysterious sentence he had written was that, of seeing the light in the room and the ghostly figures of Craig, and Sarah's grandfather wrapping his arms around her just after her last breath. Finally, he ended the

letter with what his feelings were, when Sarah died, and what he did before going out of the door. Telling also of the love he had for his sons and the hope that one day they might forgive him. When I had finished reading the letter, Daniel continued to speak to me."

"This is my daughter, Mariska, Sarah's granddaughter, she is so like her mummy. Would you like to hold her?"

"Although unspoken, I could sense his wish for me to hold this little one in place of Sarah. She was the most beautiful baby girl I had ever seen. Her black, glossy hair encompassed perfectly her sweet face, with the odd wet curl where she had been lying asleep. Her lips were perfectly bow-shaped, she had a wee snub nose and her deep brown eyes, with the long dark lashes were mesmerising. She studied my face for a few seconds with a puzzled look, then, gave me a warm, winning smile. In that moment I wondered how many hearts she would break when reaching puberty, and indeed, how stunning her mummy must be. I felt privileged to hold Sarah's granddaughter in her place.

Daniel told me of how the Authorities had finally found Craig's remains and that the family were arranging to have him buried with a befitting service. Fraser had apparently travelled back to his hometown of Aberdeen and ended his life by jumping from Union bridge. I was shocked, and began to wonder what terrible last thoughts must have been going through Fraser's troubled mind on the three hour drive to Aberdeen, and at what point he had decided to commit suicide.

There are no words I can think of, which would adequately express, the hurt, anger, and pain, that Daniel must have been feeling. Even the birth of his precious daughter must be tinged with sadness in finding his mother dead, reading of his brother's murder all those years ago at the hands of his father, and then to be told of his father's suicide. Thus, I admired greatly, his resolve when he calmly and determinedly announced."

"I know in my heart that my mum is looking down on us now and smiling."

*"A week later, while catching up with some outstanding reports in my office, and now being in possession of the full facts relating to Sarah's case, I decided to peruse Sarah's lot once again. On closing the file, I pondered to visualise a smiling Sarah. How nice it would be, to think that what Daniel had said was true, and that Sarah **was** looking down on her family, and smiling, don't you agree?*

To my mind, the three victims in this story were Craig, as the victim of murder, Fraser, as the victim of wretchedness, caused by his own making and resulting in needless manslaughter, and finally Sarah. Poor Sarah, whose only crime was that of wishing to be loved, being the victim of years of mental abuse at the hands of her husband, due to circumstances outwith her control.

Four years later, I met Daniel once more, with his baby son. He too had big brown eyes and dark hair like his sister, but looked like his daddy. Daniel showed me a video, which he had taken on his mobile 'phone, of Mariska singing beautifully, 'I'll do anything for you dear' from the film 'Oliver,' saying how much this would have pleased both Sarah and Martha. He also informed me that Anthony and Tiffany had a baby girl, and I was pleased that Sarah's youngest son and his family were happy and settled in their new home abroad. However, it was a bitter/sweet pleasure for me as I thought of Sarah's hopes for a girl in the family having been realised, with not one, but two granddaughters, and the sadness of her not having lived to know them."

FORGIVE ME JENNY

This book tells the story of Veronica who, was sexually abused by her father, as a child. Her mother, on eventually discovering this, moves with the little girl from Devon to Aberdeen hoping for a fresh start. Veronica makes friends with Jenny but develops a simmering jealousy of her as she is a pretty girl with a normal loving family, both of which she desires. Eventually Veronica moves to America after the man she loves marries Jenny. For a time she finds happiness there but her jealousy heightens when a tragic event occurs. Returning to Aberdeen, Veronica has kidnap and murder on her mind.

CHAPTER ONE

It was the year 1965 in Torquay, Devon. A man had just come out of his six year old daughter's bedroom and was closing up his trousers and fastening his belt. In the bedroom, six-year-old Veronica Adams is quietly crying into her pillow confused as to why her daddy could say he loved her but make her do such awful things. Things she did not like. This had been happening every Wednesday night for a year while Florence (her mother) was having her weekly night out with friends. Veronica did as her daddy wished in order to show how much she loved him. He had conditioned her over that time to indulge in his sexual bidding in the name of his love for her, which, being so young and innocent, she wholeheartedly believed. She had been told it was 'their secret,' and asked not to tell anyone, not even her mummy.

Veronica, a very thin little girl with jet black hair, dark eyes, thin face and a white complexion (almost ghostly), did not like herself very much and really wished she looked prettier. The fact that, she, was being sexually abused, by her father, only added to the ugly perception she had of herself. Her one and only salvation was that she loved to write short stories, and enjoyed the praise given by her teacher at school for these. She dreamed of the time when she was older, imagining herself writing a book which would have a beautiful picture on the cover, **in red**, as this was her favourite colour, then she would become famous.

On one of her Wednesday evenings out, Florence had felt ill and decided it would be best if she went home early. On arriving at her house, she unlocked the front door and entered into the hallway. She was surprised that there were no lights on downstairs. Thinking that Veronica should be asleep in bed at that time, and not wishing to waken her, she crept quietly upstairs. On opening the door to peep in and check her daughter, she was horrified, at the sight, which met her. She could see what her husband was up to and was sickened to her stomach. Immediately, she pushed him out of the room screaming at him to get out and never darken her doorstep again. The house, having been, originally owned by Florence's parents, was left to her in their 'Will', after their passing. Being as she was the sole owner, she was within her rights to tell him to leave. She then took her daughter into her arms and cuddling her close said, 'I am so sorry luv, I did not know this was happening, but don't you worry mummy's here now and I won't let anything like this happen ever again.' After tucking the confused little girl up in bed for the night, she lovingly kissed her on the cheek. As she left her daughter's room she paused to wonder just how long this had been happening to Veronica, and what lasting damage it might have on her. Little did she realise, in that moment, the extent of the unhappiness Veronica would have to endure in the future.

After going downstairs, Florence, while still shaking with anger, made up her mind to go the next day to a solicitor and start divorce proceedings. This she did but over the next few months, her estranged husband persistently kept calling and turning up at the house demanding to see his daughter. With all the raucous going on, it did not take the neighbours long to find out about the situation and subsequently, things were not going well for Veronica at school. Florence decided enough was enough and put the house up for sale intending to go as far away as possible to start a new life where no one knew of their prior history. Professionally, she was a senior nurse, who could quite easily pick up work in any hospital, as the NHS were always desperate for good medical staff. Therefore, she made the decision to move to the city of Aberdeen in Scotland in order for a fresh start for herself and her daughter

By 1969, everything was in order and Veronica was then eight years old when they moved to Gardenhead Place, in Aberdeen, where Florence had secured a nursing position at Foresterhill hospital. 'Now darling,' she said to her young daughter, 'we are beginning a new life here, so don't mention your secret to anyone!' Veronica felt alone and miserable, this was her secret and she would have to take it to the grave. It was never far from her mind, however, and would haunt her for years to come. Ironically, she still loved her daddy and in fact blamed her mummy for the fact that she could no longer see him. There was never a closeness between mother and daughter because of this, only a wide chasm. Over the coming years, Florence tried her best to resolve this situation, but found it difficult owing to the fact that she was a single parent who worked long shifts leaving little time to accord her daughter. To shut away the hurt and guilt of the little girl she was inside, Veronica had developed a quirky persona. She became a sort of rebel in the way she acted and dressed, giving the outward appearance of self-confidence. However, inside she was a frightened, fragile, little girl who craved love and had no idea what was to happen to her in the future.

Printed in Great Britain
by Amazon

51691807R00078